'Beth,' he whispered.

He was staring at her mouth, and she ached to feel his lips on hers. She swallowed to moisten her parched mouth as she swayed towards him. She mustered her last skerrick of sense. 'We shouldn't be doing this,' she croaked. 'Things are complicated enough.'

'Yes, they are,' Gabe whispered, his gaze not leaving her mouth. She was so close, her mouth so near he could almost taste her, and he wanted her so much his body throbbed.

'Can you walk away?' he asked softly. *I sure as hell can't.*

Beth shook her head, not sure she could articulate a response. His intense gaze on her mouth was breathtakingly erotic.

'Neither can I,' he groaned as he dropped his head and claimed her lips.

Dear Reader

Welcome to Brisbane General Hospital! Set in my home town of Brisbane, this trilogy explores the lives and loves of three nurses, the Winters sisters—Beth, Rilla and Hailey. And three very special doctors—Gabe, Luca and Callum.

I've always wanted to write a linked series, and was thrilled when my editor suggested it. I love catching up with previous characters and being familiar with a particular setting. And Brisbane General is a beauty. Being a nurse, I can tell you there's no place quite like a hospital to bring out real emotions and make people realise what is truly important in life.

In TOP-NOTCH SURGEON, PREGNANT NURSE, Beth never thinks she'll see the stranger she impulsively slept with again—until he turns up at work as the new hotshot surgeon. Now they have to work together in the operating theatres of Brisbane General—and despite the intense attraction she's determined to pretend it never happened. But their secret will soon be out when Beth discovers she's pregnant!

There's never a dull moment at Brisbane General. So fasten your seatbelts and enjoy the ride!

Amy Andrews

Don't miss Rilla's story in November 2008!

TOP-NOTCH SURGEON, PREGNANT NURSE

BY
AMY ANDREWS

MILLS & BOON®

Pure reading pleasure

First published in Great Britain 2008
Harlequin Mills & Boon Limited,
Eton House, 18-24 Paradise Road, Richmond, Surrey TW9 1SR

© Amy Andrews 2008

ISBN: 978 0 263 19904 8

Set in Times Roman 10½ on 13 pt
15-0708-47884

Printed and bound in Great Britain
by Antony Rowe Ltd, Chippenham, Wiltshire

Amy Andrews has always loved writing, and still can't quite believe that she gets to do it for a living. Creating wonderful heroines and gorgeous heroes and telling their stories is an amazing way to pass the day. Sometimes they don't always act as she'd like them to—but then neither do her kids, so she's kind of used to it. Amy lives in the very beautiful Samford Valley, with her husband and aforementioned children, along with six brown chooks and two black dogs. She loves to hear from her readers. Drop her a line at www.amyandrews.com.au

Recent titles by the same author:

THE OUTBACK DOCTOR'S SURPRISE BRIDE
FOUND: A FATHER FOR HER CHILD
THE ITALIAN COUNT'S BABY
SINGLE DAD, OUTBACK WIFE
AN UNEXPECTED PROPOSAL

To my dearest friend, Leah. Who knows.

CHAPTER ONE

BETH ROGERS stared at her office wall, reliving Friday night over again in all its horrifying splendour. She blew on her tea as she absently tucked a stray strand of blonde hair back into her theatre cap.

A pair of vivid green eyes, the exact shade of the peridot in her favourite pair of earrings, had haunted her all weekend. Crinkly caramel hair styled into a trendy just-got-out-of-bed fashion had continually flashed on her inward eye. A well-modulated English accent had replayed relentlessly. The aroma of popcorn, coffee and shortbread lingered even now.

How could she have done that? She'd never had a one-night stand in her life. Never.

At thirty-eight, no doubt there were some out there that would think that terribly boring. But having had her life defined by an even worse error of judgement at fifteen, she'd always shunned the casual sex scene. At least this time round she'd made sure they'd used protection.

'Here she is.'

'Where else would she be at seven in the morning, even though as NUM she doesn't start till eight?'

Beth looked away from the very fascinating wall to find her two sisters lounging in her doorway. She smiled at them, plastering an all-is-well-with-the-world look on her face and banishing those peridot eyes. 'Good morning to you both, too.'

Rilla and Hailey entered and threw themselves down on the low lounge chairs that sat against the wall opposite the desk.

'Well, I know why I'm here this early—' Beth began.

'Because you're a workaholic,' Rilla interjected.

Beth ignored her. 'But why are you both here so early?' Like she needed to ask. Rilla and Hailey had been hovering for days. 'I thought you were on days off, Rilla. And, Hailey—you don't start till one. Wet the bed?'

The sisters looked at each other. 'Come on, Beth. We're just worried about you,' Hailey said, putting all her best counseling skills into the conversation. 'We're family. When you hurt, we hurt.'

'Yes,' Rilla agreed. 'We've been fretting all weekend about you.'

Beth looked at her sisters and felt their love and concern. They were so different from her. She was lanky and blonde, like the few photos she'd seen of her mother. They were darker and curvier, like Penny, *their* mother. But she'd been part of the Winters family for over twenty years and, blood bond or not, she was as close to them as any sisters.

She shook her head and smiled at them. 'I'm fine guys, really. This is a tough time of year for me. I know you know that better than anyone else and I appreciate your concern.'

The sisters exchanged looks again. Beth's words were reassuring but they knew how bruised her heart was still, even twenty-three years down the track. Had lived through that tumultuous time all those years ago as well and even though they'd both been quite young, Beth had been unbearably sad and it had left a lasting impression.

'So did you go and see that movie Friday night?' Hailey asked.

Friday night. No, she was trying not to think about Friday night. 'Yep,' she said, hoping to sound nonchalant.

Rilla looked at, Beth waiting for more information. None was forthcoming. 'Was it able to distract you like you hoped?' she prodded.

The movie hadn't but what had happened afterwards certainly had! It had kept her distracted all weekend. 'Yep,' she said again.

Rilla and Hailey exchanged yet another look. 'I didn't think an action movie would hold your attention for long, you're more a foreign-film buff,' Rilla persisted.

'Oh, yes, all that blowing up stuff.' Beth nodded convincingly, 'very good distraction.'

'What did you do afterwards? I hope you didn't go back to your house and brood all night. You know we would have come over.' Hailey frowned, her concern all too obvious.

Yes, she knew. But she hadn't been able to bear the thought of it. Her sisters' efforts to keep her mind off the baby she'd given birth to twenty-three years go would only have served to focus her mind on it more. They'd been there to witness the aftermath of that turbulent time and their presence alone would have been enough to stir the memories.

Beth decided to throw them a crumb to sidetrack them. 'I actually walked out of the cinema into a medical emergency. A woman had collapsed into a diabetic coma and then she started to fit. This…' Beth paused slightly while she searched for an adequate description. 'Guy and I, rendered some first aid while we waited for the ambulance.'

'Guy?' Rilla and Hailey said in unison, recognising the significance of Beth's hesitation, sensing a juicy titbit.

Damn it! She shouldn't have stumbled over how to explain him. She should have known her sisters would jump on that part of the information.

'What was he like?' Rilla asked.

'What's his name?' Hailey pressed.

'What's he do?' Rilla added.

'Spill!' Hailey demanded.

Hot. He was hot. Amazing green eyes, beautiful mouth and a way with her body that had made her weep in his arms.

'He seemed nice enough,' she fobbed them off, hoping her nose wasn't growing. 'His name is Gabe. He's English. He's a teacher.' They were looking at her expectantly and she knew how tenacious they could be so she threw them another crumb.

'We had coffee.'

And he made me laugh. He made me forget. And he was flirting and he had desire in those amazing eyes and something else, something sad, and when he suggested I go back to his hotel room I did because I couldn't bear to be alone with the memories, and we had sex. All-night sex. Last-night-alive-on-earth sex. Armageddon sex. Until I slunk out of his room at dawn.

'Coffee?' the sisters said in unison again, looking at Beth speculatively.

'Do you fancy him?' Rilla asked.

Beth rolled her eyes. 'He's…younger than me.'

'How much younger?' Hailey demanded.

'Thirty-three.' But he hadn't looked a day over twenty-eight.

'So?' Hailey shrugged.

Her sister's words triggered a Friday-night flashback.

'Look, I'm flattered but you're a little young for me,' she had said and had laughed nervously.

'So?' Gabe had said, staring at her with desire and heartbreak in his eyes.

'Don't you think you should be playing with girls your own age?' she'd practically squeaked.

'No.'

And he'd been so sure of what he'd wanted and yet still kind of vulnerable, her insides had melted and she'd taken his proffered hand and followed him without any further argument.

'Is he married?' Hailey's persistent voice broke into her wandering thoughts.

Beth gave her sister a scandalised look. 'No.'

'So?' Hailey stated again.

Beth looked from one to the other, her head spinning. She was glad her instinct to keep Friday evening's full story to herself had kicked in. For as long as she could remember her sisters had been trying to set her up with men. It was their payback for years of her mothering them. But the last thing she needed was them constantly questioning her about Gabe.

She didn't want to be frequently reminded of her completely out-of-character actions. She already had a son out there somewhere to remind her of that. Her one-night-stand-man was best left at the hotel.

'So nothing. We had a pleasant chat.' Beth waited for a lightning bolt to strike her. 'He's in Australia for seven months. I'm never likely to see him again.'

'What sort of a teacher is he?'

'I don't know. We didn't really talk about our jobs,' Beth said wishing she was wearing a theatre mask to hide the heat she felt rising in her face. *She'd slept with someone she barely knew.* They'd talked about the movies and books and music. *And then they hadn't talked about much at all.*

Beth was saved any further interrogation by the arrival of the Brisbane General's Chief of Staff. She'd never been so happy to see the man who'd been more like a father to her than the man who had actually given her life.

'Ah, not one daughter but all three,' John Winters said, beaming at his girls. He didn't have to ask why they were altogether—he knew why.

'Hi, Dad.' Rilla and Hailey rose to hug their father and he gave them a big grateful squeeze each. He winked at Beth over the top of their heads. 'How are you darling?' he asked gently.

Oh, God, not you too. 'I'm good, John. Really, I'm OK.'

John moved into the office and Beth rose to embrace him. He was tall and broad and handsome still, his hair greying nicely at the sides. She lingered in the circle of his arms, thankful every day that John and Penny had taken her in and given her a second chance at life.

'To what do I owe the pleasure of your hallowed company?' Beth teased. 'It's a bit far down from the executive suites to the bowels of the hospital, isn't it?'

John chuckled and sat on the corner of her desk. 'I'm

just showing the visiting neurosurgeon around. He's meeting me here shortly.'

'Dr Fallon?' Beth asked.

'The English guy? The one who's leading the neuro team to separate the Fisher twins?' Hailey piped up. 'What's he like?'

'He has an impeccable reputation. He's only thirty-three but has a very bright future. He's worked on some real cutting-edge stuff in Oxford and has a very successful private practice. He's been involved with separating two sets of craniopagal conjoined twins already. The Fishers are lucky to have him. The General is lucky to have him.'

'That's not what she meant, Dad,' Rilla said, laughing at her sister.

John's eyes twinkled. He'd known exactly what his youngest daughter had meant. 'Well, he doesn't do much for me but I guess you young things would call him a hottie. Why, interested?'

'No way,' Rilla said vehemently. 'But Beth, on the other hand...' she turned to look at her older sister '...needs a good man.'

'Hey!' Beth protested. 'If anyone needs a man around this joint, it's you. It's about time you started moved on. It's been seven years since Luca left.'

'Absolutely,' Hailey agreed.

'You can't talk,' Rilla said turning to her younger sister to deflect the attention from her. 'How long has it been for you?'

Hailey laughed. 'Give me a break. I only got back into the country eight weeks ago.'

'You're normally faster than that,' Rilla pointed out.

Hailey started to protest and then figured it was a little

rich to be outraged by her sister's comment when it was essentially true. She'd had a string of boyfriends. But things had changed in London. 'I'm mellowing in my old age.' Hailey shrugged.

They all laughed and Hailey joined them. It was good to be back home among the family again. She'd missed them on the other side of the world and their familiarity was like a soothing balm to her burnt-out soul.

Dr Gabriel Fallon heard their laughter all the way down the corridor. He looked up at the sign that jutted out from the wall above the door where all the noise appeared to be coming from. It read 'O.T. Nurse Unit Manager.' Definitely where John had told him to come. *Looked like the Brisbane General was going to be a fun place to work.* It would make a nice change from the gloom he'd left behind in England.

He approached the office and knocked quietly on the door. John was sitting on the desk, two women were sitting in the chairs against the wall and another, behind the desk—John's daughter, he presumed—was obscured from his view by her father.

'Am I interrupting something?'

Beth felt the laughter die a sudden death on her lips. That voice. That accent! She'd know it anywhere. The same voice that had asked her to his hotel on Friday night. The same voice with the sexy accent that had whispered outrageous things to her all night.

'Gabriel,' John said, rising to his feet and ushering the newcomer inside. 'Pardon us. Clan gathering. Meet my daughters. This is Rilla. She's the middle child. She works down in Accident and Emergency.'

'Rilla.' Gabe nodded extended his hand. 'A pleasure to meet you.'

Beth watched Rilla blush under Gabe's gaze and knew exactly how she felt. His accent flowed over her like warm icing on a hot cake. *Oh, God, oh, God!* What the hell was he doing here? Gabe? Teacher Gabe? Her Gabe was the new hotshot from the UK? No wonder he'd been so good with the diabetic. *First-aid course, my fat eye!*

'This is Hailey, the youngest child. She's just started on the kids' ward. She's been away for three years in your neck of the woods.'

'Oh, whereabouts?' Gabe asked, shaking her hand.

'London,' Hailey confirmed.

Oh, God, it's me now. Beth wished she could hide under the table as she watched her father and Gabe turn towards her. Time ground to a halt as their actions appeared to unfold in slow motion.

'And this is the woman in charge around here. She's also done quite a bit of travelling and even worked in Oxford. This is my oldest daughter—'

Gabe's eyes widened as recognition dawned. 'Beth!' he supplied before John had a chance.

Gabe couldn't believe what he was seeing. The woman who'd been on his mind all weekend was standing in front of him. Her hair may be obscured by a cap, her lithe body covered in baggy theatre greens, but he'd remember that flawless complexion, those eyes, that mouth anywhere. *Hell!*

Beth swallowed, trying to moisten her suddenly parched mouth. Nothing had prepared her for the impact of seeing him again. On Friday night he'd worn jeans and a polo shirt. Today he was wearing dark grey trousers, a striped business shirt and an impeccably matching tie. But she knew neither were a match for what lay beneath.

'Hello, Gabe.'

John frowned. 'You two know each other?'

Intimately. Gabe had thought about no one else since he'd woken alone in his bed on Saturday morning. He'd slept with the boss's daughter? A colleague? *Oh, good move, Gabriel!* He saw a burst of panic flare her pupils and her blue eyes darted nervously to John and then back to him. *She didn't want her family to know.* 'We…met on Friday night.'

Beth could see Hailey and Rilla exchange looks in her peripheral vision as his green eyes captivated her, making it impossible to look away.

'You're the guy who helped her with the diabetic?' Rilla exclaimed.

Among other things. Gabe smiled at Rilla and then turned back to Beth. 'Yes. We made quite a team.'

John was looking at Beth and she quickly filled him in with an abridged version of events, ignoring the familiar undertone in Gabe's voice.

'Well, then. No introduction needed,' John said.

Gabe saw a slight hint of pink adorn Beth's high cheek-bones. *Definitely no introduction needed.* He wondered if John Winters would have been so welcoming had he known just how well acquainted he was with Beth.

'It'll be a pleasure working with you,' Gabe said.

Beth nodded, unable to speak, trying not to focus on the word 'pleasure'. Was it just her hyperactive imagination or had he emphasised it slightly? Her body was still tingling in places from the pleasures they had shared.

No! This couldn't be happening. If she'd known she was going to have to work with him, she would never have thrown common sense and a lifetime of caution to the winds and slept with him. The one thing, the only thing, she'd managed to comfort herself with over the weekend had been she'd never have to see him again.

'Well, we'd better be getting on,' John said. 'I believe Dr Fallon has an afternoon list, Beth?'

Beth looked at John and nodded. She forced herself to concentrate on only him, ignoring both Gabe's and her sister's speculative. 'Starts at one.' She leafed through some papers on her desk and handed one to Gabe.

'Thanks,' he said softly as he took the theatre list. He watched her intently as she avoided his gaze. 'I guess I'll see you after lunch.'

Beth gave him a quick smile, which she hoped appeared friendly, and made a show of straightening the papers on her desk. Rilla and Hailey were shrewd. Too shrewd. If she ignored him, started acting weirdly, they'd be onto her. She could tell they were already bursting to get her alone.

John gestured for Gabe to exit first. 'See you later, girls.' John smiled at his daughters as they left the office.

Beth sat, her shaky legs dubiously supportive. She adjusted a few things on her desk and then risked a look at her sisters. They were looking at her with grins on their faces.

'What?'

'You didn't mention that Gabe was so gorgeous,' Rilla stated.

'Very sexy,' Hailey concurred. 'Slip your mind?'

'He's OK, I guess.' she shrugged.

'You guess?' Hailey laughed. 'That man is so damn cute I thought about slipping into a diabetic coma just to grab his attention.'

Beth grinned at the image and then sobered. 'Well that man is now apparently a colleague so the rest of it doesn't matter.'

'Thought you said he was a teacher?' Hailey said.

Beth shrugged. 'That's what he told me.'

A great start to their working relationship. Not only had they slept together but he'd lied to her. Had the flirting and flattery been lies too? To get her into bed? He had confessed to her, as they'd eaten from room service at three in the morning, that he'd never done anything so spontaneous before. Had that been another lie?

She had suppressed the impulse to question him further at the time knowing that a few hours in bed with a stranger did not permit her access to the intimate details of his life, and now wished she hadn't. She'd known what had driven her to act so outrageously—what had been his excuse?

Beth groaned inwardly. What did his reasons matter? The more important question was how she was going to work with him. The next six months stretched before her interminably and she wished they were over already.

'Well.' Rilla grinned and winked at Hailey. 'Looks like Gabe's going to be around for a while. You never know what could happen in that time.'

Beth looked from one to the other. Their brown eyes sparkled mischievously at her. 'No.'

Rilla and Hailey's grins widened.

'No,' Beth repeated, more emphatically this time.

'Oh, come on, Beth,' Hailey cajoled. 'I think he fancies you.'

Beth tried not to remember just how much he'd fancied her on Friday night. 'I'm not interested.'

'Liar, liar pants on fire,' Rilla teased.

'I do not date colleagues.'

'Oh, Beth,' Rilla chided. 'You do not date, full stop.' She made a chicken noise and flapped her arms a couple of times. Hailey giggled.

Beth fixed her sister with a glare. 'Rilla, you of all people should know how disastrous relationships at work can be.'

Rilla's smile died and Hailey's laughter cut off abruptly. Her sisters looked at her as if she'd slapped them, and Beth knew she'd stepped over the line. *Damn Gabe Fallon!* She'd done nothing but mother and dote on them since she'd entered their lives twenty-three years ago. Rilla had been seven at the time and Hailey five.

'I'm sorry, Ril,' she said immediately, getting up from behind the desk and crouching beside her sister's chair. 'I spoke without thinking.'

Rilla blinked and smiled weakly. 'It's OK, Beth. I know you didn't mean it that way. Just because it didn't work out for me, it doesn't mean they're necessarily a bad thing. You have to stop punishing yourself. It's been twenty-three years…'

It was both incredible and daunting to have two other human beings who knew everything about you and loved you anyway. Who knew what kind of ice cream you liked or what you wished for when a falling star crossed your path or how you'd cried yourself to sleep for a year. Despite their physical differences, despite their different surnames, Hailey and Rilla were her family. She didn't know what she'd do without them.

Beth looked into Rilla's earnest brown eyes. She took her sister's hand and gave it a squeeze. She reached for Hailey's and did the same.

'Listen, guys. I love you both but I don't need fixing up. I like my life. I have a great job and my own place and I can do what I like, when I like. I'm happy.'

Beth knew it was hard for her younger sisters to grasp. They were both still at an age when marriage and children were possible. Two years off forty, she'd given up on the often desperate need to hold a baby in her arms and her dreams of becoming a mother again. And she'd mourned that for a while but in the last couple of years had found some peace with it.

'Now, come on, you two,' Beth said, breaking away and standing up. 'Thanks for coming but go away now. I have work to do.'

Rilla and Hailey stood and they all huddled together for a group hug, their foreheads touching.

'You could just use him for sex,' Hailey suggested. 'He looks like he'd know some pretty slick moves.'

Rilla burst out laughing and Beth joined in despite shaking her head at Hailey. *You have no idea, sister, dearest!*

'Goodbye you two.' Beth kissed both her sisters and returned to her desk, pleased to be alone again.

She put her head on the desk and groaned. Now what? How was she supposed to see Gabe every day and act like she hadn't seen him naked?

The day got worse. Kerry Matthews, her second in charge and the scrub nurse rostered to work in Theatre Four with the new neurosurgeon, went home at lunchtime with a migraine. The other two nurses allocated to the theatre were junior and as such had had little experience in neurology cases.

Beth had cut her teeth in neurosurgery. She'd worked for two years at the internationally renowned Radcliffe in Oxford when she'd first gone traveling, and had been working there again when she'd come home for Rilla's wedding eight years ago and decided not to go back.

So, with the other theatres staffed and running smoothly, Beth resigned herself to having to scrub in. She stood at the washbasins outside Theatre Four and put her mask on. She could do this, she thought briskly as she tied the paper straps. Just hand him the instruments as he asks for them and try and anticipate his needs. Nothing she hadn't done for any other surgeon in the past eighteen years.

Except she'd never slept with any of the surgeons she'd worked with. And it wasn't like she hadn't had her share of opportunities. Because she had. *But she didn't do that.* She didn't sleep around. At all. And certainly not with colleagues.

Sure, there had been some relationships. But her past had made her very reserved and distrustful so nothing had been successful for long. And no one had got past the detached veneer to the softness beneath.

Letting that go long enough to let someone in was a big step for Beth. Too big. It meant giving up some hard-won control and that terrified her. Too many things had happened in her younger years that she hadn't been able to control. Being fostered by the Winters had put her back in charge of her life and it had been the gift she'd treasured most from her new family.

Beth flicked the taps and pushed the surgical scrub dispenser with her elbow. Green liquid squirted into her hand and she began the three-minute routine she could perform in her sleep, trying not to think about having to stand close to Gabriel Fallon for the next few hours.

'You ran out on me.'

Beth started. She hadn't heard him approach. The hairs on the back of her neck stood to attention as his presence loomed beside her. She turned her head to see him lounging against the sink, applying his mask. Looking at her.

'Yes.' What else could she say?

'I was hoping to...have a late breakfast. Maybe make a weekend of it.'

Beth faltered in mid-scrub. A whole weekend in bed with Gabriel Fallon. The mind boggled.

'You lied to me. You said you were a teacher.'

Gabe turned to face the sink and flicked the tap on. 'I do a little lecturing.'

Beth glared at him over the top of her mask.

Gabe chuckled. 'Look. I'm sorry. I don't usually tell people I'm a neurosurgeon. I'm good at my job but it takes up so much of my life. I have a killer schedule and I so rarely get the chance to socialise. When I do, I like to keep my work at work. And it can get weird. People know you're a doctor and they always want a consultation.' He scrubbed at his soapy hands for a few moments. 'Would you have stayed if I'd told you I was a neurosurgeon?'

She could hear the smile in his voice and she didn't have to look at his peridot eyes to know they'd be laughing. Beth snorted. 'I wouldn't have gone to bed with you if I'd known you were a neurosurgeon.'

He nodded as he scrubbed at his wrists. 'I'm glad I was...economical with the truth, then.'

Beth worked the soap down towards her elbows, ignoring the way the mask muted his voice, accentuating the accent, making it sound husky as hell.

Time for a few home truths. 'I don't do one-night stands.'

He'd known that the minute he'd suggested she go back to his room. He could still recall how totally shocked she'd looked for those seconds before something had changed in her eyes and she had taken his hand. 'I never intended it to be a one-night stand.'

'I don't do two-night stands either,' she said primly, horrified by the leap her pulse took at his statement.

He laughed and the noise caused a flutter inside her and she scrubbed harder at her arms. 'This is not funny. This is a disaster.'

Gabe frowned. 'No, a disaster would have been if we'd slept together and it had been awful. And it wasn't.' He looked down at her and their gazes clashed. 'It was good. It was very, very good.'

Beth heard her breathing go all funny. She couldn't refute it, no matter how much she knew she had to get this conversation back on an impersonal level.

She cleared her throat and turned back to concentrate on her scrub technique. 'Be that as it may, we have to work together for the next seven months so I think we need to establish some ground rules.'

Gabe smiled behind the mask. 'This should be good.'

'One. Forget Friday night happened.' She looked at him for confirmation.

He nodded.

'Two. No references to Friday night—ever.'

Gabe nodded again.

'Three. Be professional at all times. I will call you Dr Fallon and you will call me Sister Rogers. Four—'

'Rogers?' Gabe interrupted, frowning. 'I thought John said you were his daughter? Oh, God…you're not married, are you?' She hadn't mentioned a husband and she hadn't been wearing a ring. Maybe that's why she'd looked so panicked?

'No!' Beth said indignantly. Did he really think she would have slept with him had she been married? 'John is my foster-father. I've been with them since I was fifteen.'

Gabe struggled with relief and curiosity. 'Ah. I see,' he said, even though he didn't really.

Beth pressed on. 'Where was I?'

'Number four, I believe.'

Beth nodded. 'Four. No fraternising outside work—'

'Look, Beth, let me spare you the rest of the list,' Gabe interrupted. 'I happen to agree. Relationships at work should be avoided.'

Not that it was a strict rule for him. He'd had relationships with colleagues before but they'd always known the score. Relationships with women who didn't, women like Beth, were to be avoided at all costs.

'I have no intention of continuing where we left off. I live on the other side of the world. I'm here for seven months only. There would be very little point.' *Except for the pretty amazing sex, of course.* 'You have no need to fear. I will be nothing but professional.'

'Good.' Beth held her arms up under the tap and let the water run down them from her fingertips to her elbows, sluicing the soap off. 'We're both on the same page, then.'

She shut off the taps with her elbow and waited for the excess water to drip off her arms squashing the traitorous flutter of disappointment at his easy capitulation. She flapped her arms, briskly to dispel it altogether, keeping her arms bent. And then she turned on her heel, her now sterile arms held out in front of her.

Gabe watched her go, pushing open the theatre doors with her shoulder, her green theatre scrubs accentuating the length of her thighs and the slimness of her hips and bottom. He shook his head as he watched the last drips of water fall from his elbows.

That morning Beth had been thrown but this afternoon she'd been back in control. All business. Where was the woman who had struck such a chord with her sad eyes on Friday night? Who had come apart in his arms? Who had wept as she had come down from the heights they'd climbed?

Something had been up with Beth Rogers on Friday night. Maybe it had been his own recent grief that had made him sensitive to her inner turmoil but something had made her act completely out of character. Impulsively. As had he.

He'd known after about five minutes in her company that she wasn't the type to sleep with a virtual stranger. And yet after her initial shock she had followed him willingly—surprised the hell out of him—and given him everything she had.

He could still hear the gut-wrenching quality of her sobs as she had curled herself into a ball beside him. There had been such misery in her outpouring. Heartbreak and sorrow and grief. It had come from something buried deep inside. And, with his own emotions still a little raw, it had affected him more than he wanted to admit.

Beth Rogers was certainly a conundrum. Not that he had the time or the inclination to find out what made her tick. She was right. They were colleagues and he didn't need any complications messing with his burgeoning career. Separating conjoined twins was complicated enough.

He flicked off the taps and drew a mental shutter on their one-night stand. He had an aneurysm to clip.

CHAPTER TWO

Two weeks later, Gabe was staring down at the eight-month-old Fisher twins, lying back to back in their pram, fused occipitally. He was still amazed at the rare phenomenon. One in two hundred thousand live births. And craniopagus? Only two per cent of Siamese twins were joined at the head.

Most doctors could go a whole lifetime and never see this condition but in his relatively young career he'd now seen three sets of craniopagus-conjoined twins and had successfully separated two of them. Consequently, he was one of the world's foremost experts.

As the late, great Harlan Fallon's son, the world had expected big things of him, and fate, it seemed, had intervened to ensure that Gabe's career was just as stellar as his father's had been. A tremor of excitement ran through him. In approximately four months he could give these precious babies separate lives.

He hoped. Gabe was aware, more than anyone, of the pressures that were being put on him to ensure a third successful operation. With two positive outcomes under his belt and the Fallon reputation at stake, failure wasn't an option—despite the enormous odds against him. But he'd faced long odds twice already and won. Looking down at the girls now, he hoped his luck wasn't about to run out.

Bridie babbled away while her sister slept. She smiled a dribbly smile at him and he offered her his finger, which she grasped willingly.

'She likes you,' June Fisher commented.

'Well, I do have a way with women,' he joked as he allowed Bridie to suck his finger.

'Oh, yeah, you're real big with the babes.' Scott Fisher grinned.

Gabe laughed and they chatted some more about the op. 'As I explained earlier, the most important thing we can have on our side is time. We'd like to wait until Bridie and Brooke are at least ten kilos before we operate. It's a big operation and we want them to be as strong as possible. Brooke is almost there but her sister...' He stopped and smiled down at Bridie '...is still lagging behind. We'll get the dietician involved and hopefully she should be bang on target for her first birthday.'

'That'd be a great birthday present for them,' a teary June said. 'To be able to see each other for the first time.'

Gabe repeated his warning that while they would do everything they could, it was a long, risky operation and there were no guarantees. They could lose one or both of the girls. Or even if they both survived the rigours of the operation, one or both of them could have brain damage. He was particularly worried about Bridie. Her sluggish weight gain indicated she wasn't as strong as her twin.

'The team's going to be spending these next four months practising every step of the operation. I have all the scans, the MRIs and the angiography, and we have 3D images as well as several plastic models of the girls' heads we're working with so when we come to operate, every step will have been rehearsed.'

Gabe had been consulted in the Fisher case since their birth and, thanks to the wonders of the internet, had been involved with the planning right from the start.

'I want you to come along to the weekly case conferences we'll be having. It's important to me that the whole team meets both you and the girls so we can all get to know each other. It'll be a good forum for any questions you may have too.'

Scott nodded. 'Of course. We'd love to get to know the people who are going to be involved in the girls' separation. Thank you for involving us. You've been great, disrupting your life and career in the UK. We can't thank you enough, Gabe.' He gave his wife's hand a squeeze.

Gabe smiled. 'Don't thank me yet. The other thing we need to think about is that, despite everything, we may have to go for an emergency separation if something unforeseen happens.'

'Yes, we've been told that's a possibility,' Scott said.

Gabe nodded. 'It's obviously something we want to avoid. We want to be able to control as much of the situation as possible so the girls get the best outcome possible. If we have to go for an emergency separation it'll be because one or both of the girls' health is failing, and that's not an optimal condition to be operating under. So keep doing what you're doing. Feed them up and keep them healthy.'

Gabe chatted with the Fishers for a little while longer and then held open his office door as June manoeuvred the pram out. He waved at them as they walked away, shutting the door as they disappeared round a corner. Two lovely people, parents who would go to the ends of the earth for their children—he hoped he didn't let them down.

He stood looking at the scans illuminated on the viewing box. The enormity of the task ahead was staring back at him. Two separate but fused brains, tethered together by networks of wispy fibres.

It would take hours, at least twenty if everything went successfully—many more if it didn't. And involve a team of about thirty people. Several other neurosurgeons, plastic surgeons, vascular surgeons, anaesthetists, radiographers and nurses.

And that didn't take into account the hours of treatments and scans they'd already endured. A month ago plastic surgeons had implanted tissue expanders under the scalps around the operative site. Every week the twins had came back to have saline injections into the expanders so the skin would be nice and stretched and able to be closed over the gaping surgical wound that would remain after the separation.

Gabe switched off the light and removed the scans. He checked his watch. Three o'clock. His outpatient clinic was over for the day. He had time to go down to Theatres and get some more practice in on the Fisher twin model.

He entered the male staff change room and climbed into a set of theatre greens. He donned a blue hat and tied it securely in place at the base of his skull and covered his shoes with the slip-on bootees made out of the same thin, gauzy material as his hat.

He passed Beth's office but noticed she was talking to

a group of people and didn't stop. Their relationship had been cordial, strictly business, their night together a taboo subject. Which was just as well. Neither his career nor the Fisher twins could afford the kind of distraction that could flare out of control should they ever cross that line again.

Except as he snapped the scans in place on Theatre Ten's viewing boards, he realised he did think about her and their night together an awful lot. Too much. Even now, while he was trying to concentrate on the intricate meshing of Bridie and Brooke's cerebral vasculature, his mind was wandering to the room down the corridor.

Damn it! He turned away from the scans in disgust. In a few short months, maybe less if they were unlucky, he had to separate the intertwined circulation—he needed to focus!

Gabe was good at focus. Focus had got him to where he was today. One of the world's foremost neurosurgeons. And at work his mind was always on the job. Always. He was driven. Career orientated. Focused. Nothing distracted him. Certainly no woman. And he couldn't let that happen now.

His father had reached the pinnacle of transplant medicine by never letting anything divert his attention. Not a wife or son or colleagues or a reputation as an arrogant, pompous bastard. Thousands of transplant patients had benefited from the advances Harlon Fallon had pioneered and that was the most important thing. If ever Gabe had felt neglected or had yearned for a little attention, he'd remembered the Nobel Prize his father had won.

His father had made a difference to the course of modern medicine. And that's what he wanted to do. He wanted to be to neurosurgery what his father had been to organ transplantation. And before his death his father had been proud of him. But he couldn't rest on his laurels. He'd gained an impressive global reputation, now it was his job to build on it.

Beth stared at the four student nurses standing in front of her. They looked terrified. She remembered how scary and overwhelming it had been when she'd first been sent to the operating theatres as a student and softened her words with an encouraging smile.

She was giving them her usual spiel about her high standards and what she expected of them. The operating theatres were a dynamic environment where one mistake could have serious ramifications—one careless miscount, one accidental contamination of a sterile field. She needed them to be vigilant.

They all looked impossibly young. They were second years. The three young women didn't look twenty. The young man looked slightly older, maybe twenty-two or three. *The same age as her son.* Her heart ached just looking at David Ledbetter. He was tall and blond with a dimple in his chin, and she found herself wondering for the millionth time what her own son would look like before she ruthlessly quashed it.

'OK, then. Time for a tour. Go round to the change rooms.' Beth pointed to the door through which they'd entered. 'Put on a set of greens, a pair of bootees and a cap and then knock on my door.' She pointed to the door on the other side of her office that led into the theatres.

The four of them stood there, looking nervous. 'Now,' she prompted.

The students darted from her office and Beth relaxed.

For a moment she wished she could be one of those NUMs that she heard the students talk about with affection. The ones who smiled a lot and befriended their students. But she was a little too reserved for that. Her background had taught her to be wary. Detached. So a reticence to get too close or involved was almost second nature to her.

Although Gabe hadn't had any problems getting past her reserve.

And it was difficult to be chummy when she had to ride them over their sterile technique and lecture them on the necessity of the endless cleaning required to keep the ultra-clean environment of the operating theatres as pristine as possible.

Her job required that she be a perfectionist—patients' lives depended on it. It was up to her to set standards and see they were maintained. And in the operating theatres, the standards had to be highest of all. Sterility and safety were paramount and the buck stopped with her. There was no place in her theatres for sloppy standards. And everyone who worked in the OT knew it.

Beth had struggled for years over how to bridge the gap between the person she had to be and the less reserved, more outgoing one she'd like to be. And in the end she'd given up. The people who mattered, who had known her for a long time, knew the real Beth beneath the guarded exterior. And she was fine with that.

There was a knock at the door and Beth opened it, stepping onto the sticky antiseptic mat which removed any dirt that had dared to venture into her office and stick to the bottom of her clogs. She gave a brisk nod of acknowledgement.

'This is the main theatre corridor,' Beth said, looking up and down, launching straight into it.

'Down this side are a couple of offices, the staffroom, change rooms and storeroom. On the other side...' she pointed to the swing doors of Theatre Five opposite '...are the ten theatres.'

She strode down the corridor. 'The theatres are not to be entered from these doors we see here but rather through the anaesthetic antechamber.'

Beth walked through an open doorway into Theatre Eight's antechamber. 'The patient is put under anaes-thetic and intubated in here.' Beth indicated the monitor-ing equipment and stocked trolleys. To the left a double swing door separated the operating suite from the an-aesthetic area.

She walked through the antechamber and under another open doorway. 'This is the room where the surgeons and scrub nurses scrub up.' The room housed a line of four sinks and it too had a closed swing door to the left which led into the theatre.

'This door,' Beth said, walking past the sinks to the far side of the scrub room, 'leads to the equipment corridor.' She pushed the single swing door open and indicated for the students to precede her. 'Basic supplies are kept here. It's also where the trays of instruments are sterilised prior to each procedure.' Beth stopped at a large steriliser fixed to the wall, its door open.

'At the end of the procedure, after all the instruments have been accounted for, the instrument trays come back out here and are passed through this window,' Beth pointed to the small double-hung opening behind the students.

'You lift the window, place the tray on the bench and shut it again. This puts the instruments in the hands of the nurses who run the dirty corridor beyond the window. This is the area where the instruments are cleaned, the trays reset and then sent to the central sterilising department.'

Beth drew breath and looked at the students, who all looked like their heads were about to explode with information overload. She saw the lost look on David's face and her heart went out to him.

'It's OK,' she said, taking pity on them. 'It's a lot to take in now but you'll soon get the hang of it.'

It didn't seem to help. None of them looked convinced so she kept them moving back out to the main corridor.

'There are ten operating suites. Two are usually kept free for emergency operations. Today that's Theatres Eight and Ten. This afternoon in the other suites we have three general surgery lists, two orthopeadic lists, an ENT list, one Caesar list and one gynae. Tomorrow you can go in and observe cases.'

Beth noticed the lights ablaze in the tenth suite as she approached. 'This is not acceptable,' she muttered as she strode towards it. 'I try to run these theatres as efficiently as possible. These big theatre lights are hellishly expensive to run,' she lectured. 'Lights must always be out if the suite is not in use.'

Beth entered the anaesthetic area, making a mental note to talk to Tom, the head theatre orderly, about it. It was the orderly's job to do end-of-day cleaning and that involved turning the lights off.

She veered to the left and shoved the double swing doors open with a shoulder, the students following close behind.

Gabe looked up at the interruption to his concentration.

He'd been engrossed in a particularly tricky vessel dissection and was annoyed at the intrusion. Especially as it was thoughts of the woman in front of him that had made it difficult for him to get into it in the first place.

'Oh.' Beth stopped abruptly.

Neither of them said anything for a moment.

'I'm sorry, Dr Fallon, I didn't realise you were in here.'

Gabe gritted his teeth at her formality. Despite agreeing to the necessity for it, he longed to hear her say 'Gabe' again, like she had that night. 'That's quite all right, Sister Rogers. I was just working on the Fisher case.'

Beth nodded. 'I'm showing some student nurses around. They'll be with us three days a week for the next six months.'

'Ah,' Gabe said, loosening a little. He never missed an opportunity to teach. 'They might be here when we separate the twins.'

'The Fisher twins?' Joy, one of the students, asked.

Gabe smiled at her. 'Yes. Come over here. I'll show you the scans.'

Beth stood back a little while Gabe explained the unusual anatomy and answered the students' eager questions. A little too eager, Beth thought. If the girls batted their eyelashes any more they were bound to fall out. Not that she could blame them. The combination of his well-modulated voice with his touch-of-class accent was hard to resist. He should have been working for a phone-sex hotline. His voice stroked all the right places.

'How often are you practising?' David asked.

'I try to do a little each day,' Gabe said. 'But we're having our first multi-disciplinary practice here on Saturday.'

He looked at Beth and she gave a brisk nod. Not something she was looking forward to. Seeing him every day was hard enough, without having to spend hours in his company on what should have been a day off.

'We're starting at eight,' she confirmed.

'And what does the practice entail?' David asked.

'Saturday is mainly big-picture stuff,' Gabe said. 'The logistics of the amount of people involved. Trouble-shooting and contingencies if things don't go according to plan. We have a weekly case conference starting Monday to discuss the intricacies.'

'How many staff will be required on the actual day?' Joy asked.

Beth almost rolled her eyes at the way the student nurse was preening in front of Gabe. She was a pretty redhead with a cute nose and an even cuter spray of freckles across it. Gabe shot her a smile and Beth couldn't suppress the frown that wrinkled her forehead.

'The cases I was involved with in the UK had about thirty personnel helping in one way or another during the separation process.'

Beth could tell each of the students was hoping to get a look-in. 'I'm sorry,' she said to them, 'only the most ex-perienced staff will be on the team.'

Gabe nodded. 'Sister Rogers is right. With so many var-iables, so much potential for disaster, we need to have only the most skilled people.'

The students asked a few more questions. 'OK, I think we need to let Dr Fallon get on,' Beth broke in, checking her watch. 'We'll continue our tour.' She paused at the door, looking back over her shoulder. 'Don't forget the lights when you're done, Dr Fallon.'

Gabe's gaze met hers. *Business as usual.* 'I won't, Sister Rogers.'

Beth shook off the intensity of his gaze as she took the students to the recovery unit next, explaining the set-up and routine post-op monitoring. She didn't get too detailed. There would be more for them to see and learn next week and she could tell they had already overdosed on information. Before sending them on their way, she handed out their workbooks and briefly explained the competencies they'd be expected to achieve while here.

It was nearly five o'clock when Beth sat back down at her desk. All the lists except for Theatre Three's had finished for the day and Recovery was emptying. She should have gone home an hour ago but she was due at John and Penny's place for the regular weekly Winters family meal and decided she'd work on the roster for an hour and go straight from work to tea.

The roster was the worst part of her job. With ten theatres to staff and eighty nurses to appease, someone was bound to miss out on their requests. She always tried to be fair with the weekend and on-call shifts but invariably she managed to alienate some of her staff.

There was a knock on her door. 'Come in,' she called, not bothering to look up from the spreadsheet on her computer screen.

'Have you got a moment?'

Beth's head snapped up. She hadn't expected it to be Gabe. How was it that the man even made a pair of plain cotton theatre scrubs look good? 'Certainly, Dr Fallon.'

Gabe's brow wrinkled. 'Really, Beth, is it necessary to

continue with such formality when we're alone? I have seen you naked, remember?'

Beth gasped. 'Do you mind?' She got up from her desk and shut the door as images of a naked Gabe filled her mind. 'Yes, it is necessary, Dr Fallon. At work, it's imperative.'

The truth was, Beth was scared stiff that if she called him Gabe, everyone would know they'd slept together. That there would be a betraying catch in her voice that would give her away. 'Gabe' had been what she'd called him when he'd been inside her. 'Gabe' had far too many intimate connotations for her to bandy it around with any ease.

'And I would appreciate it if you didn't use "naked" in any sentence when talking to me.'

Gabe sighed as he lowered himself into a chair opposite her desk. Beth's office smelled of her. The same fragrance that had stayed with him since they'd first met. Like cinnamon doughnuts and a citrus orchard. Whatever it was, it overrode the pervasive antiseptic smell that invaded the operating suites.

'OK then, Sister Rogers…no "n" word. Whatever. I was wondering if you'd given any thought to rostering the nursing team for the big day.'

Beth was relieved he'd dropped the subject and had gone straight to talking shop. Her heart was still galloping madly as she tried to follow his train of thought. 'I was going to look at that on Saturday. I know who we need, it'll be a matter of who's available when the date's chosen.'

Gabe nodded. 'I'm thinking we should set a tentative date. That will help with staffing in all departments.'

'Even if we can narrow it down to an approximate week. If we're looking at four months from now, that's May,'

Beth scrolled through to her annual leave spreadsheet. 'I'll have to rearrange some things. A couple of my most experienced staff are down to take leave during that time.'

'Yes, OK. I'll look at trying to set an estimated date. Will that help?'

Beth nodded briskly, trying to be businesslike when that chair had never been filled so well in all its life. 'I take it you'll want to do this on a weekend? We'll be needing so many staff we won't be able to run other theatres as well. It would leave them too short.'

'Yes, logistically it's the only way to do it,' Gabe agreed. 'Of course, that's in a perfect world. If we need to go to an emergency separation, that could happen on any day.'

Beth nodded. 'We may have to cancel some cases if that happens. Is it likely?'

Gabe rubbed his jaw. 'Bridie is definitely the weaker twin. She's not thriving like her sister. They're both in good health at the moment but if Bridie picks up a bug and can't fight it off, she could jeopardise Brooke's health too. It's a possibility.' He gave her a smile that was half-grimace. 'I guess we have to cross that bridge if we get to it.'

Beth saw a flash of vulnerability in his green gaze and realised the enormity of the job that had landed in Gabe's lap. Sure, the surgery would require a team effort, but he was the leader, the 'expert'. The outcome, good or bad, would be on his head.

She felt a rush of tenderness welling inside her as she remembered the carefree man she'd slept with. How different was the man before her? Dr Gabriel Fallon was an entirely different animal to Gabe, her Friday-night man.

She remembered the first day she'd scrubbed for him,

Dr Gabriel Fallon, eminent neurosurgeon. She'd been worried how it would work so closely on the heels of their one-night stand, but she needn't have been. He'd all but ignored her, demanding perfection from her and everyone in the theatre. Treating her with the utmost in professional courtesy. As if their fling had never happened.

So different from the Gabe of their first meeting. Gabe, the lover. Sure, she hadn't been able to shake the feeling that something hadn't been quite right with him that night either, and he'd all but confirmed that when he'd admitted to his spontaneous behaviour, but he'd still been relaxed and laid back.

And if the whispers she'd heard since about his reputation were anything to go by, that Gabe enjoyed a party and a flirt and the company of women who knew the score.

Beth supposed the pressures of his work almost demanded this type of split personality. His job was highly stressful so it seemed only sensible to release the pressure through playing jack the lad in his downtime.

She opened her mouth to say, It'll be all right, Gabe, then caught herself in time. She pressed her lips firmly together. She didn't want to be part of his downtime. Best not to give him any encouragement.

'Fingers crossed, we won't.' Beth stood. 'Was there anything else, Dr Fallon?' she asked primly.

Gabe contemplated saying something shocking just to rattle her. Beth was one single-minded woman. 'No, Sister Rogers.' He stood also. 'I'll consider myself dismissed.'

Beth watched him go wishing it was just as easy to dismiss him from her thoughts.

* * *

The sun was setting as Beth pulled up at the Bullimba house she'd called home since she'd been fifteen. Her gaze took in its rambling whitewashed exterior. It had been a palace compared to some of the dives she'd lived in on the streets and she'd loved it the second she'd clapped eyes on it.

She was running a little late. She'd done battle with the roster for another hour and then given it up as a bad joke. Gabe's scent, sweet like shortbread, had invaded every corner of her office, making a mockery of her concentration. She'd stopped at the nearby shopping centre and picked up a bunch of flowers for Penny.

Beth walked up the path and was raising her hand to insert her key in the lock when she heard a car door slam behind her and a sexy voice say, 'Wait…'

Beth's heart crashed against her ribs as she turned towards the voice. 'What the hell are you doing here?' she demanded.

Gabe laughed. 'That's no way to speak to a dinner guest.'

He was wearing the clothes he'd worn to work this morning. Chocolate-brown trousers and a purple pinstriped shirt. The tie had been removed, the top buttons undone.

'I hope your family are drinkers,' Gabe said as he drew level with her, holding up a bottle of wine.

His crinkly caramel hair was still a little flat from his theatre cap and despite her absolute horror when she realised she would be sharing the table with him, she suppressed the urge to ruffle it. 'You're having dinner with us?' *Great. She'd drink the entire bottle all by herself!*

Gabe nodded. 'I ran into your father on my way out of the hospital.'

Damn John. 'No,' she said, shaking her head. 'You can't have dinner with us.'

Gabe chuckled. 'Yes, I can. John asked. I accepted.'

'But…Dr Fallon—'

'Beth,' Gabe said sternly, 'I swear to God, if you call me Dr Fallon all evening…'

'Sorry Dr…er…Gabe.' Beth tried not to stumble over the word but she did anyway. 'Look, you don't understand. It would make me feel very uncomfortable.'

Gabe frowned. 'Why?'

She stared at him for a few moments, wondering whether he'd lost his mind. 'Because we slept together,' she said, lowering her voice to a harsh whisper. 'Or have you forgotten that already?'

He grinned at her, remembering in vivid detail. 'So?'

So? So! So she couldn't exchange polite pleasantries with him in front of her family and not give herself away. 'Rilla and Hailey are very shrewd. They'll guess. And I don't need them on my case. They'll try to matchmake and it was a one-off G-Gabe. A one-off. Not to mention that my father is your boss. You want to be sitting across the table from him when he realises just how well you know me?'

Gabe could see the pink in her cheeks as her straight blonde hair brushed her shoulders. He sighed. 'How old are you Beth?'

Beth glared at him. 'Older than you. Old enough to know better than to jump into bed with a complete stranger.' *How could she have been so stupid?*

'I don't care who knows that we slept together, Beth.'

'Well, I do,' she snarled. 'What happened with us is not the way I act. I'm embarrassed by it. I'd like to keep it to myself, if that's all right. I'm worried we might slip up and let the cat out of the bag, especially if we're together socially with my family. They know me too well.'

'Beth, what happened between us wasn't exactly normal for me either. We were both acting out of character. There was something obviously weighing on you that night. Don't forget, I held you while you cried your heart out. It meant something to me that you could let go. Whatever you think, it was more than just a one-night stand.'

Beth shut her eyes. She could hear the sincere note in his voice and wished he hadn't reminded her of how she had broken down. The fact that it apparently meant something to him she couldn't even begin to process.

'Please…' She opened her eyes and fixed him with pleading eyes. 'If it really meant something then I'm asking you to just turn around and leave. I need to be more prepared than this.'

Gabe saw the desperation in her eyes and a hint of the sadness that had afflicted her that fateful night. He handed her the wine and opened his mouth to agree.

The door opened abruptly. 'There you are. Both of you,' John boomed. 'Well, don't just stand there, come on in. Penny is so looking forward to meeting you.'

Gabe shot Beth an apologetic look as he allowed John to usher him into the house.

Beth stood staring after them, wine bottle in one hand, flowers in the other.

Damn it!

CHAPTER THREE

To MAKE matters worse, Penny sat Gabe and Beth together. She was super-aware of him as they took their places at the table. His body heat radiated towards her, stroking hot fingers across her skin. The occasional brush of his arm against hers caused unwanted flashbacks.

Rilla and Hailey sat opposite, grinning at her. She frowned at them. John and Penny sat at each end of the table, oblivious to any odd vibes.

'So, where in the UK are you from?' Penny asked.

'I grew up in Reading. My mother still lives there. I studied in London. But I live in Oxford at the moment.'

'Oh, Beth worked at the Radcliffe in Oxford for years, didn't you, darling?' Penny supplied.

'It was a long time ago,' Beth said evasively.

'How long have you been back for?' Gabe asked.

Beth concentrated on Penny's divine roast lamb. 'Eight years.'

'Beth's been all over,' Rilla boasted.

It was true. Beth had left on her travels as soon as her training had been complete. Being welcomed into the loving arms of the Winters clan had been her saving grace but memories of her baby boy had haunted her and she'd been desperate to escape them. A decade of wandering the world had helped put them into some perspective.

'How long have you been theatre NUM?' Gabe asked politely.

'Five years.'

Gabe could tell from her tight replies that she'd rather he didn't talk to her. Knew that she'd rather he wasn't here at all. And he did plan on eating his meal and leaving but it seemed rude to ignore her in the meantime.

As if he could have anyway. Given their close proximity, his body was excruciatingly conscious of hers. Every movement she made brought her body into contact with his and he was reminded of the way her skin had felt on *that* night.

'So, Hailey, you've been to the UK too?' Gabe asked, smiling at Beth's younger sister.

Beth let out a relieved sigh and let the conversation flow around her, participating only when required.

'Are you OK, Beth?' John asked, as he stood to clear the dishes, 'you seem very quiet tonight.'

Beth could see the concern in the older man's eyes and could tell he was anxious about the recent anniversary. She gave him a reassuring smile. 'Just preoccupied by the Fisher case. There's so much to organise.'

As Penny served dessert the conversation swung to the case that had captured worldwide media attention.

'You must be under a lot of pressure, Gabe,' Penny said. 'Two successful separations under your belt is quite an impressive precedent.'

Gabe shrugged. 'I suppose so. I try not to worry about

other people's expectations though. My own are high enough.'

'What are their chances, do you think?' John asked.

'It'll depend very much on their shape going into the operation. If we can get the twins to the ten-kilo mark and Bridie and Brooke are healthy, their chances will be much better.'

'And if everything is as you hoped?' John pressed.

Gabe really hated predicting outcomes even though he knew it was the one thing people most wanted to know. Certainly Scott and June were eager for the figure. 'Two healthy girls going in still only gives them about a fifty per cent chance of both of them pulling through. It's a massive operation...too much potential for catastrophe.'

'How does it compare to your other cases?' Hailey asked.

'Well, all three sets of twins have been joined in different parts of their heads so in essence each operation is completely different. I think the Fisher case, however, looks the most technically difficult.'

'Oh, I so hope those little girls pull through,' Rilla said softly.

'Yes,' Hailey agreed. 'They're quite a fixture on the kids' ward. Scott and June pop in for a visit every week when they come to the General. The twins are always so happy and placid, they have this dear thing they do where they hold hands. It's so sad that they're joined at the backs of their heads and can't see each other.'

Gabe had thought so too. 'Well, hopefully they'll be able to look into each other's eyes before much longer.' Gabe smiled. 'I'm going to do everything in my power to make it happen.' *And Fallons didn't fail.*

'So I guess you two will be working quite closely on this?' Penny asked. 'It seems like a mammoth task.'

'We will need to be co-coordinating a lot,' Gabe confirmed, sensing Beth tense beside him.

Gabe caught the speculative look Beth's two sisters exchanged out the corner of his eye. She was right—they didn't miss much. He was struck by how similar they were. Rilla and Hailey were definitely Winterses. Both short and curvy with dark hair and olive skin like Penny's.

Tall, blonde, peaches-and-cream Beth shared no similarities whatsoever. If he hadn't already known that Beth was John's foster-child he'd have begun to suspect the milkman may have had a hand in her conception. Differences aside, there was a lot of obvious love around this table and he felt an unreasonable spike of jealousy needle his chest.

The Winterses personified the type of family he'd always yearned to be part of as a child. Growing up in a household that had been torn apart by his father's slavish devotion to his job, it had never occurred to him that families with a medical background could actually be functional. Certainly his father had always been at pains to drum into him that dedication to medicine and family did not mix. That you could have one or the other. But not both.

And yet he was sitting amidst the living proof that his father had been wrong. John Winters was a successful doctor at the pinnacle of his career. The chief of staff of one of Brisbane's largest hospitals was a very powerful position indeed. And yet he obviously loved his girls, had a great wife and made time for his family. It could be done.

He glanced at Beth, still tense beside him. He felt a

strange urge to reach out and pull her into his side. Rub his hand along where her neck sloped into her shoulder. Knead the tension away. For the first time ever in his life he was seduced by the idea that it was possible to have both. Medicine and a life. Maybe even be more successful with the support of a loving a family.

'Have you scheduled any team practice sessions yet?' John asked.

'Saturday morning is our first,' Gabe replied, looking away from Beth, pulling himself back from his fanciful thoughts. *One hour at the Winterses' dining-room table, sitting next to Beth, and he was forgetting years of hard lessons.*

He sat up straighter. 'We also have our first case conference on Monday morning which involves Scott and June and the girls.'

'How often will the surgical team get together to practise?' Penny enquired.

'That's something we'll need to discuss on Saturday. Once a week at least for the whole team or as much of the team as possible. It'll depend on everyone's schedules, which is why it'll happen on a weekend. No doubt there'll be a lot of smaller group practices going on too. The case conferences will be weekly.'

'Sounds like you'll all know your stuff by D-Day.' Penny nodded. 'It's a good idea really, for team bonding as well. An operation of such magnitude surely requires not only a well-oiled but a close-knit team. Getting to know and trust each other would be paramount.'

Beth, who had been wishing the conversation to end, blushed, thinking about how well she knew Gabe.

'Absolutely,' Gabe agreed. 'The team needs to have a

familiarity with each other and be united towards our common goal.'

Familiarity? Beth dipped her head as she reddened further. They were already too familiar. Their familiarity was carnal!

'Well, good luck. No doubt Beth will keep us up to date and you must come and have tea with us again. Coffee, Gabe?' Penny prattled as she cleared the dessert plates.

Oh, God no. Just go, please, go. Sitting next to him as he talked, their carnality pulsing between them, was shredding her composure. His accent flowed over her like warm butterscotch and every cell in her body demanded she rub herself against him and purr. She could have sworn he had been about to touch her a little while back. She was getting a crick in her back from sitting so straight.

Beth desperately willed him to decline. She looked at him directly for the first time all evening, a plea in her eyes.

Gabe recognised it immediately. Her hair framed her face and her steady blue gaze begged him to leave. She needn't have bothered. Being at the Winterses' was playing havoc with all his previously held opinions. He wanted out too.

'No, thanks, Penny. Actually, I think I might head off now.' He made a show of checking his watch. 'I need to ring one of the Hopkins neurosurgeons in the States and discuss the case.'

Penny and John pressed him to stay, but beside him Beth's relief was almost palpable. He declined and stood to go, thanking Penny for the invitation.

He bade farewell to Rilla and Hailey. 'I guess I'll see you tomorrow,' Gabe said, looking down at Beth's erect posture.

Beth nodded, acutely aware of him standing behind her, his heat almost a physical caress.

'Tomorrow.'

John and Penny showed Gabe out and it was only when she heard the door click shut that she sagged against the chair.

The Saturday morning practice session came round too soon. Beth arrived at seven and tackled the problem of how to staff the operation while she waited for the others to arrive.

There was no scheduled lists today, just emergency cases, so the theatres were running on a skeleton staff. More nurses were on call should extra be required. She could hear laughter drift down the corridor from the staff-room as she pondered the personnel required and how to give them all adequate breaks during an operation of inde-terminate length.

By eight the key players had arrived and they all assem-bled in Theatre Ten. It was the largest operating suite and, as such, equipped to cope with the numbers that would be required on the day.

Today there were four neurosurgeons, two plastic surgeons, two vascular surgeons, two anaesthetists, four nurses and two orderlies. Sixteen people. It was expected there would be almost double that number on the actual day. And theatre ten already seemed too small.

It was a busy morning. They discussed the logistics of the surgery and managing the number of people. Various issues and potential problems were aired and everyone suggested ways these could be overcome. Gabe was a fount of knowl-edge, drawing from his experience, able to troubleshoot and identify areas that no one else had thought of and employ-ing some of the solutions they'd used in the UK surgeries.

They talked over the best ways to manage all the

equipment needed and did a dummy run, one of many they'd do between now and the operation, involving shifting one of the twins to the other table once the separation was complete.

Beth was also keen to set a procedure in place early for emergency resuscitation. The surgery was obviously hugely risky and she wanted everyone involved to know the resuscitation procedure back to front just in case. Gabe was able to advise how they'd managed in the UK and between them they came up with a quick, efficient way to deal with the worst-case scenario. Everyone would know their role in such a situation before the operation even began.

Beth's head was spinning by the time they called it a day four hours later. She had lists of things she needed to organise and follow up. Extra lighting, sufficient of instruments and regular practice days were the most pressing.

Having the theatre fitted with closed-circuit cameras was also something that needed to be sorted out sooner rather than later. Gabe had insisted on the importance of such a set-up. On D-day the tearoom, which would act as the main hub for superfluous staff, would have live footage relayed to its screens so everyone could keep abreast of the progress.

Beth knew that a lot of modern theatres were being built with these systems already in place. One of the newer south-side hospitals had all its theatres fitted out and she made a note to talk to the NUM involved about the intricacies of the system.

They agreed to meet every Saturday as a team and the surgeons would practise the exact techniques both alone and together in addition to the whole team sessions. Beth felt a bit like she was training for an Olympic event except there were more than medals at stake. Two precious lives depended on them. Penny was right—how did Gabe cope with the pressure?

'We're all going to the pub for lunch,' Kerry said as she popped her head into Beth's office. 'Join us?'

Lunch with Gabe? Tea had been bad enough. 'I want to get some of this organised,' Beth said waving her list in the air and picking up the phone.

'Oh, come on, Beth,' Kerry cajoled. 'You work too hard. Have lunch and then come back afterwards if you want.'

Beth looked at the pleading look on her friend's face. They'd known each other for a long time. 'I'll join you later,' she fobbed her off, knowing she wouldn't be doing anything of the sort. 'You going to Barney's?'

Kerry nodded. 'You'd better or I'm going to send Gabe over to drag you here.'

'What am I going to do?' Gabe asked, popping his head in too.

'Beth's passing on lunch.'

Gabe looked at Beth and then back at Kerry. 'Leave it with me. Save us both a space.'

'No,' Beth said, when she'd given Kerry enough time to be out of ear shot.

Gabe sighed. 'You know, Penny was right. We do need to be a well-oiled team. This operation is a hugely stressful event. Socialising will help build rapport and it gives us another forum to discuss the operation. Maybe talk about things we hadn't thought about.'

'Take notes,' she said, and started to dial a number.

Gabe entered her office and pushed the call cut-off button.

'Dr Fallon...' Beth gaped.

'Sister Rogers. I'm afraid I'm going to have to insist. Debriefing is mandatory.'

Beth tried to ignore how her skin erupted with goose bumps at his insistence. His accent slid over her like silk and she felt a pull down low in her abdomen.

They glared at each other for a few moments. Beth looked at his finger still firmly in place. This was ludicrous. There was a huge group of them, she didn't have to talk to him at all.

'Let me make a few phone calls and then I'll join you,' she finally acquiesced.

Gabe smiled at her as he lifted his finger. 'Thank you.' He strolled towards the door. 'If you're not at Barney's in thirty minutes, I'm going to take Kerry up on her suggestion.'

Beth swallowed as his silky threat tantalised more than it terrorised.

Twenty-five minutes later Beth stopped at the kerb, waiting for the green man. She looked to her right. The city sky-scrapers loomed nearby. The General had been around for over a century and whoever had chosen this spot had done well. It was prize real estate, with its city views and prox-imity to the hustle and bustle of downtown Brisbane.

The light changed and Beth crossed the busy road, heading towards the garish neon sign that announced the pub's location. Barney's was a popular hangout for the hospital staff, being situated as it was directly opposite the General.

She stepped into the jovial atmosphere and moments later squinted into the dark recesses as her eyes adjusted from the bright sunshine outside.

'I was just about to come and get you.'

Beth wasn't expecting the sexy low threat growled in upper-crust English so close to her ear and her skin tingled where Gabe's breath fanned her skin.

'We've ordered fish and chips,' he said, ushering her along with him as he balanced three beers. 'What do you want to drink?' he asked, as everyone greeted her and he pulled out her chair.

'Um…' Beth was still catching her breath from his earlier statement. 'Chardonnay, please.'

She listened, slightly dazed, as the conversation flowed around her. Any chance she had of forming coherent chatter died as Gabe joined her, plonking her wine on the table in front of her and sitting down next to her.

He joined in the flow easily, unlike Beth who had developed a sudden case of muteness as her awareness of him rose to excruciating levels.

He was dressed as Gabe. Laid-back Gabe. Not the cool professional he'd been an hour ago, dressed in scrubs and a cap, concentrating and focused on the Fisher case, calling her Sister Rogers. He was in jeans and a polo shirt like he'd been the first time they'd met. His caramel hair looked like it had been carelessly finger-combed, making him look impossibly young, and he was smiling at her. A lot. And calling her Beth.

Oh, god! Despite telling herself not to, despite not wanting to, she had a thing for him. She took a gulp of her drink. How embarrassing. Hadn't she embarrassed herself enough in front of him? Not content to just sleep with him after five minutes' acquaintance, she'd also sobbed like a baby in his arms. Beth took another gulp of her wine. Coming here today had been a mistake.

She was grateful when the meal arrived and people concentrated on eating instead of talking.

'So,' Gabe said, his voice low. 'I enjoyed my time with your family the other night.'

Beth cringed, thinking about how his surprise invitation had thrown her and how uncomfortable she'd felt sitting next to him. She'd been less than polite. 'John and Penny enjoyed your company,' she murmured, trying to make amends for her behaviour.

'Only John and Penny?' Gabe teased.

Beth glanced up from her meal at him and saw his easy grin. She ignored him, returning her attentions to her beer-battered fish. His ego didn't need any massaging.

'How old were you when the Winters fostered you?' Gabe asked.

Beth stopped in mid-chew. 'Fifteen,' she said stiffly.

Gabe noted her reticence. 'I'm sorry. I'm prying. You don't like to talk about it.'

Beth placed her cutlery on her plate carefully. 'Not at all. I just don't see the point in discussing it.'

Gabe laughed. 'It's called conversation, Beth. You know, social interaction? Getting to know each other? We seemed to have put the cart before the horse and I thought it might be nice to get to know each other beyond the…physical.'

His voice lowered on the last word and she shivered. Like she needed reminding of their uninhibited beginning. Talking about her past seemed preferable to hushed references of their night together. 'It's a long story. My mother died when I was six—'

'I'm sorry,' Gabe interjected.

Beth shrugged. It wasn't as if she remembered her. The

only images of her mother she could recall had come from battered old photos. 'I didn't really know her.' Except that wasn't entirely true. Vague, elusive sensations of being hugged and rocked and loved were never far away.

Maybe if her mother hadn't died, the rest of her life wouldn't have gone to hell. And her father would never have insisted she adopt the baby out. But, then, if she'd lived there'd have been no catalyst for the dramatic downward spiral and life would have been very different. Beth probably wouldn't have found herself in the predicament in the first place.

'My father… Things were bad after. He threw himself into his work, shut me out. I think it was too painful to acknowledge me. He was distant and the times he wasn't he was harsh and critical. He remarried. My stepmother… well, she wasn't exactly…kid friendly. I rebelled in my teenage years. We fought a lot. The stricter he got, the more I rebelled. After years of ignoring me he didn't know how to handle me.'

Gabe listened to her tale of woe and could draw eerie parallels with his own life. He was beginning to see why Beth was so reserved, so tightly in control of her actions. Her childhood had been fraught. He remembered how his own parental circumstances had buffeted his life and the constant state of anxiety he'd lived in for such a long time.

'I ran away.' She shut her eyes as the awful isolation and dread of life on the streets revisited her. It had been a harrowing time. She opened her eyes, stirring from the memories, realising she'd given away more than she'd meant to. 'Anyway, I eventually wound up in the foster-care system. And got lucky.'

Gabe wasn't fooled by her quick wrap-up. Somewhere there was a chunk of the story missing. Could it be worse than what he'd already heard? What had happened to her after she'd run away? Had she got into drugs or crime or other things that street kids became embroiled in?

'You certainly did,' he agreed, knowing he'd pushed too much for one day.

But there was more to the Beth Rogers story, of that he was sure. Having this glimpse into her life seemed to throw up more questions. Her uncharacteristic act of sleeping with him seemed even more peculiar, knowing what he now knew. Was there an even bigger demon in her past?

They ate in silence for a few moments. Low conversation buzzed around them. As the silence stretched between them Beth's awareness of him trebled. At least conversation kept her mind off the sensations stroking her skin.

She took a swig of Dutch courage and looked at him. 'What about you, Gabe? What was it like growing up with the great Harlon Fallon?'

'It wasn't dull.'

Beth noted his clipped reply and frowned as a memory flashed a warning light in her head. *Oh, God! Open mouth, insert foot.* 'Damn. Sorry, Gabe. He died just recently, didn't he?'

Gabe felt the heaviness in his chest that had been with him since his father's death intensify. 'A few months ago.' He nodded.

His voice sounded so bleak and Beth saw the same sadness she'd caught a brief glimpse of that first night. So…he had been grieving too. 'Look, sorry, forget it. I didn't mean to pry either.'

Gabe gave her a sad smile. 'It's OK, Beth. I don't mind talking about it.' He forked a chip into his mouth and took a swallow of his beer. 'My parents divorced when I was twelve. Dad was never around and I guess Mum got sick of being a single parent. They argued a lot. Mum accused him of loving his job more than us.'

'Ouch.'

Gabe nodded. 'Unfortunately, Dad didn't disabuse her of it. She married again shortly after. Like you, my step-father and I never really saw eye to eye.'

So Gabe had his demons too. Maybe that explained her rash attraction to him that fateful night? Maybe she'd rec-ognised a kindred spirit, had identified with his grief and been drawn to him? She looked down at her empty plate. 'I think it takes someone much stronger than a mere child to accept someone new into the picture.'

He nodded. 'I guess I felt it was betraying my father to accept Ronald. We argued a lot. I'm afraid I wasn't very nice.'

Beth remembered back to her own tumultuous teens. She hadn't been nice either. In fact, she'd gone off the rails big time. Being emotionally isolated from her father, she'd felt acutely the loss of the mother she'd never even really known. Was it any wonder she'd wound up pregnant when she'd been so hungry for some love and attention.

'Did you go live with your dad?'

Gabe snorted. 'Dad didn't have time for anyone, never mind a sullen teenager.'

Poor Gabe. The bitterness she heard in his simple state-ment was achingly familiar to her. Gabe had obviously felt as let down by his parents as she had by hers.

'So you didn't really get on with your dad either? Did you reconcile before he died?'

'I don't know about reconcile. I lived with him when I went to med school in London. He was a complex man. I don't think he'd have let me in even if he'd lived to be a hundred. But I think he was…proud of me…at the end.'

'I'm sure he was,' Beth murmured. She took another sip of her drink, leaving Gabe alone with his memories for a minute.

'Well, you must have been the envy of all your fellow students. Living with the great Harlon Fallon. You must have learnt so much from him.'

'Oh, yeah. I learnt single-mindedness. That any distractions to your career were to be avoided at all costs. That you could be a great doctor but you couldn't be a great father or a great man as well, and you had to make the choice early on. That success comes at a cost to your family.'

Beth stopped chewing. It sounded so bleak. At least the Winterses had shown her that children, even surly teenagers, needed love and had showered her with it. Thankfully she'd had a chance to be a part of a real family. A chance to start over. 'That sounds dreadful.'

Gabe smiled down at her. 'No. It wasn't that bad. I thank him actually. My father may not have been the warm and fuzzy type but in his own way he was looking out for me. He was right—doctors have one of the highest divorce rates of all professions. Surgeons are worse. Neurosurgeons worse again. None of the marriages of my friends who are surgeons have made it past a couple of years.

'Being a product of divorce has helped me prioritise in

my life. I don't think you can have the type of career I want and have a family also. That's just not fair to them.'

Beth looked into his steady green gaze, his accent oozing rivers of sensation all over her, and felt completely horrified. She had a thing for a guy who'd been raised by a robot! Harlon Fallon may have been a brilliant physician, taught his son focus and the importance of a career, but had he ever put his arms around Gabe and told him that he loved him?

She felt absurdly like doing that just now. Not the love thing. But just hugging him. Hugging the lost little boy somewhere inside who just wanted his father to love him. Maybe it was the loneliness of her early years or more likely the unrequited mother in her, but she sincerely hoped that anyone, regardless of what they did for a job, could see that family was more important than anything. Above career. Above accolades. Even above Nobel Prizes.

At least, despite all evidence of her past, she still believed that a happily-ever-after was out there for everyone. Who knew? Maybe it was still out there for her. *If she could ever forgive herself enough to love.* And it could still be out there for Gabe too. As long as he didn't become a chip off the old block.

CHAPTER FOUR

MONDAY morning the majority of the team gathered in a clinical support office on the tenth floor for the first case conference. Subsequent meetings would only involve the main players but Gabe had wanted everyone involved to meet the Fishers at least once. He wanted them to see that through all the hype, all the media coverage, this was what it was about. Two little girls. A family. He wanted to put a human face to the mammoth task that lay ahead of them.

The large room was dominated by a huge oval table and a magnificent view of the Brisbane skyline but when June Fisher pushed the pram through the doors, all eyes were on Bridie and Brooke. Those who hadn't seen the girls before, including Beth, stared in awe. They were truly a sight to behold.

Gabe introduced the team and Beth was impressed he'd remembered everyone's name even down to Tom the orderly.

'Hi.' Beth smiled at June, holding out her hand as Gabe got to her. 'I'm Beth Rogers. I'm the nurse unit manager of the operating theatres.' June and Scott shook Beth's hand. 'If you have any questions at all as we go along this morning, make sure you let us know. You two are as much a part of this team as anyone else.'

'Thank you,' June murmured.

Beth's gaze was continually drawn to the twins as the surgeons discussed the logistics of the case with their parents. Bridie was asleep but Brooke babbled away as she sucked furiously on a rattle. How Bridie slept Beth had no idea. Her sister's vocalising filled the whole room and the surgeons kept stopping in mid-sentence to smile at the happy, normal noises coming from a far from normal child.

The longer she spent in the meeting, listening to all the complex issues, the more she admired the Fishers resilience. There'd been a lot of gossip in the hospital and reports in the media that the Fishers had been irresponsible and should have had the twins terminated when their condition had become evident.

But looking at the two dear little girls Beth knew it couldn't have been that clear cut for Scott and June. Having given up a child herself, Beth knew the terrible gut wrench of such decisions. She didn't envy them their position or judge them for their choice. And none of it mattered now anyway. Bridie and Brooke were here. That was all that mattered.

Bridie started to stir and Brooke automatically reached back to touch her sister. Beth felt a lump in her throat as she watched the innate gesture of comfort. She thought about her relationship with Rilla and Hailey. About their sisterly bond and how strong it was. They *had* to pull both the girls through. After such a close tie, how could either be whole without the other?

Gabe sat opposite and she looked up to find his gaze on her. He was talking to the vascular guys and quickly turned his attention back to them but he'd definitely been watching her. Goose-bumps pricked her skin as his voice washed over her, and Beth found herself wishing they'd started off on a different footing.

It still felt awkward to be around him. She knew—she hoped—that with time and distance it would ease, but the Fisher case was throwing them very much together, not giving her the space she needed to look at him with indifference.

Scott and June departed with the girls half an hour into the meeting, along with most of the team. Beth stayed on and took necessary notes as they pertained to her and her staff's role, conscious as ever of Gabe.

When would it stop? She hoped and prayed that by the time the op came around in four months or so she'd be feeling less on edge around him because the separation would require nerves of steel. There would be no room for this odd jittery feeling. This heightened awareness of him. Gabe seemed perfectly cool with it. Why the hell couldn't she?

Two weeks passed. Two more case conferences. Beth had spent the morning away from the theatres, first attending the case conference and then travelling across the city to the Raymont Hospital to look at the way closed circuit cameras had been implemented into their theatres.

Her head was buzzing with information as she stopped by the cafeteria located in the grounds of the General, to pick up a cappuccino and a sandwich. The twins and the impending operation were uppermost in everyone's thoughts. At least Beth was finally starting to feel a little less like she had 'Gabe Fallon and I slept together' tattooed on her forehead as preparations continued.

He still had the ability to make her breathless from a smile or one word in his smooth accent but he was professionalism personified, focused to the point of obsession about the operation, and it made it easier to put their intimacies behind her.

Beth paid for her food and was passing the tables located outside, her mind on the projected budget John had requested, when she was interrupted.

'Beth.'

Gabe had seen Beth approach as he sat at a table with Scott and June and the girls. He'd run into them when he'd popped down to get some lunch and they had asked him to join them. It was a gorgeous sunny February day and he'd been more than happy to sit with them and soak up some sunshine. Februarys in England were never like this.

'Beth,' Gabe called again, louder this time as she appeared to have not heard him. He'd managed to persuade her that they could revert to first names without giving any secrets away.

The budget figures disappeared into the ether as Beth turned her head towards Gabe's voice as if pulled by a powerful magnet. She spotted him sitting with Scott and June and he waved at her. He looked all sexy and relaxed in a green shirt almost the exact shade of his eyes, a smile making his features even more deadly. Her step faltered. Did she really have to socialise with him? They were together more than was good for her sanity anyway.

But the Fishers were smiling at her and it would be rude to ignore them. She plastered a smile on her face as she approached.

'Do you guys live here?' Beth teased as she drew close.

'Feels like it.' June laughed. 'We had some other appointments and stopped for lunch. We managed to persuade Gabe that a pasty Englishman needed a bit of sunshine.'

Beth joined the laughter. Gabe was a far cry from pasty and they all knew it.

'Have you got time to join us?' Gabe asked, patting the bench seat beside him.

Beth looked at her watch, wishing he hadn't put her on the spot. She shrugged. 'I don't have to be anywhere for half an hour.'

Gabe scooted over and Beth sat. Beside her the twins babbled away in their pram, the visor down to shade them from the midday sun. Beth's eyes were automatically drawn to them as she unwrapped her sandwich.

Two perfect babies. If she hadn't known about their conjoined condition, she'd have thought they were normal babies lying back to back. They were gorgeous. Little bow mouths and blue eyes. Their fused heads were covered in a light smattering of blonde hair and Brooke had a small brown birthmark on her forearm.

'Do you have kids, Beth?' Scott asked.

Beth looked up. How many times had she been asked this question in her life? How many times had it cut her to the quick to deny it? 'No,' she said, taking a bite of her sandwich, feeling the same emptiness she always felt.

They made small talk as they ate, mainly about the girls. It was easy to think of them as one child but Beth and Gabe laughed as June told funny stories about their individual traits. As she finished her coffee Beth had a much better appreciation of the Fisher family and the challenges they faced with the girls' rare condition.

Scott and June were such lovely people. They could

have been bitter about the hand fate had dealt them but they were continually upbeat and unwaveringly positive.

'I know people think we should have terminated the pregnancy,' June said, expertly scooping the girls out of the pram onto her lap. 'But how could we have not known our girls? Even if just for a little while?'

How indeed? Beth knew too well the ache inside from empty arms. She stared at June as she kissed the girls' heads and snuggled them in close, feeling envious. June looked as dedicated and loving as any mother and Beth felt a painful twinge in her chest.

'You followed your heart,' Beth said quietly, wishing she'd had the strength to follow hers.

Gabe heard the wistful note in Beth's voice and was surprised to see a shimmer of tears in her gaze before she blinked them away. The urge to squeeze her hand was surprisingly strong. *Damn it.* Despite knowing he shouldn't be, couldn't afford to be, he was attracted to her.

Luckily for him her reserve and painstaking professionalism made it easy for him to keep a lid on it. But seeing her like this, all soft and…vulnerable, not guarded, he felt it flare out of control. Her mouth was soft and her teeth were pressed into her bottom lip and he remembered how great her mouth had felt under his. How vulnerable she'd been, sobbing in his arms.

'Would you like to hold them?' June asked Beth.

Beth knew she shouldn't. It would be breaking every professional boundary that existed but she felt so bereft at the moment and her arms ached to hold them. And they were babies. The best nurses knew that sometimes boundaries were there to be crossed.

Beth nodded and June stood to hand them over, placing them effortlessly in Beth's lap. Their smell was the first thing that filled her senses and, smiling, she shut her eyes and inhaled their sweet fragrance as she rubbed her cheek against the soft down covering their heads.

'They like that,' Gabe murmured.

Beth opened her eyes to find Bridie smiling a dribbly smile at him. Gabe offered his index finger and Bridie grasped it gleefully. Gabe laughed and Beth felt it go right to her pelvic floor muscles.

He looked up and smiled at her.

'She likes you,' Beth said huskily. Did he have the same effect on the entire female population?

'What's not to like?' Gabe grinned and returned his attention to Bridie.

Indeed. A voice that purred. Mesmerising eyes. Sexy as hell. And a hit with babies. A very dangerous combination.

'You're both naturals.' Scott smiled.

Except she was too old and he was too career orientated. Beth shut her eyes again, revelling in the feel of the two squirming, sweet bundles pressed against her. *She still wanted this.* Damn it. Twenty-three years later, her arms still ached to hold a baby.

Her pager pealed and Brooke jumped. Scott and June laughed as Beth apologised. 'I'd better go,' she said reluctantly as she pulled the pager off her waistband and checked the message.

'Here, give them to me,' Gabe said, holding out his arms.

Beth baulked at the intimacy but after one last cuddle shuffled them onto Gabe's lap and bade everyone a hasty goodbye. Unfortunately, the mental image of Gabe with the two little girls cuddled against his chest stayed with her for hours.

A few days later, due to staffing problems, Beth was standing gowned up next to Gabe, trying not to remember how right he'd looked holding the twins. At least the awkwardness she'd initially felt in his company had started to dissipate and, looking around the theatre now, Beth doubted anyone could tell from their body language that they'd been lovers.

It certainly couldn't be told from Gabe's. He was every inch the neurosurgeon as he concentrated on excising the tumour from the anaesthetised patient's brain. His movements were precise, his touch impersonal, his requests businesslike. She was taking her cues from him and it got easier every day, but part of her still expected someone to point the finger at any moment and expose them.

Beth handed Gabe a swab and noted she was running out.

'More swabs,' she requested, lifting her eyes to David, who was hovering nearby. The students had been allowed to undertake scout nurse duties this week.

David located a packet and carefully opened the sterile packaging, his finger accidentally brushing the corner of the swabs.

'Your hand contaminated the sterile field,' Beth said firmly. 'Get another packet please.' She wasn't angry, just matter-of-fact. It happened a lot, even to seasoned professionals.

But she noted the colour in David's cheeks when he returned. 'It's OK,' she said in a low voice as he opened the new packet with trembling fingers. 'It happens to the best of us. The important thing is to be honest when it happens and realise that sterility is what's important—not ego or pride. This patient needs every one of us to be vigilant.'

David nodded and performed a count of the swabs with her. She watched as he changed the count sheet to reflect the additional pack.

Beth turned back to Gabe. A sudden wave of dizziness assailed her. Her vision blurred and she blinked to clear it as she steadied herself against the table. Nausea slammed into her and she felt sweat bead on her brow. She took a few deep breaths but the mask hindered her and made her feel claustrophobic.

It took a few seconds for the light-headedness to dissipate. She became aware of Gabe asking her for something.

'Beth?' Gabe frowned, looking down at her. 'Are you with us?' he demanded.

Beth blinked and gave her head a slight shake to clear the lingering fog. 'I'm sorry,' she apologised. 'I was… thinking ahead.'

Gabe nodded, not totally convinced. 'Needle holder,' he repeated.

Beth passed it to him and leaned heavily against the table as another wave of dizziness hit. Gabe said something and she looked at him but she couldn't hear the words for the ringing in her ears and her pulse hammering madly through her head.

'Beth?'

Beth continued to stare at him as her vision started to blacken from the outside in. *Oh, God, she was going to faint!*

'Gabe,' she said breathily, before her sight went altogether, 'I think I'm going to faint.'

Gabe could see the spark in her eyes fading and it took a couple of seconds to realise that Beth was teetering on the edge of consciousness.

'David! Catch!' Gabe ordered as the unsuspecting student passed behind them.

A startled David turned just in time to catch Beth as she slumped and fell backwards. The whole theatre stared at the unconscious Beth. The very capable Sister Rogers fainting? Impossible!

'Is she OK?' Gabe demanded. 'How's her pulse?'

David placed two fingers against her neck, locating the strong, steady thump of Beth's carotid. 'Good.'

Gabe felt a wave of relief wash over him. He hadn't realised he'd been holding his breath. 'Tom, help David with Sister Rogers,' he told the orderly. 'Get her on a gurney.'

Gabe, satisfied that Beth had just fainted, shut down his concern and returned his focus to the operation. 'Which one of you is going to scrub?' he asked the three nurses standing against the wall, still looking askance at the spectacle.

'Come on, come on,' he demanded. 'Concentrate, everyone, we have a head to close.'

And with that, the operation got back on track.

Beth came to as Tom and David were placing her on the gurney the tumour patient had been wheeled into the theatre on.

She murmured and then her eyes fluttered open. Tom and David's blurry features swam before her coming into slow focus. 'Wh-what happened?'

'You fainted,' David said.

Beth blinked. Huh? Her? Faint? She'd never fainted in her life! She struggled to sit up and immediately felt woozy.

'Whoa there,' Tom said, placing a steadying hand on Beth's shoulder as she swayed drunkenly. 'I'll put the head up.'

He used the handle at the side to adjust the gurney and lift the top to bring Beth into a supported sitting position.

'I'm fine, I'm fine,' Beth protested, as she shut her eyes to stop the room spinning. 'It's probably just my blood pressure.'

David pulled the blood-pressure cuff off the anaesthetic monitor and placed it around a protesting Beth's arm.

'Eighty on forty-five,' he announced when the figure appeared on the monitor.

'See,' Beth said crankily. 'Just a bit of postural hypotension.' Except she really felt like she was going to throw up.

'I've known you since you did your training here, Beth,' Tom said sternly. 'You are not a fainter. Everything all right?'

Beth nodded firmly. 'Of course. I think maybe I just need to eat something. My blood sugar might be a little low.' Beth swung her legs round until she was sitting on the edge of the gurney, pleased that the dizziness had settled.

Tom nodded. 'I'll give you a hand to the tearoom.'

Beth squared her shoulders and looked the orderly, who had been at the General since before her father, in the eye. 'You will do no such thing, Tom Lester. I'm perfectly capable of walking unaided.'

They helped her off the trolley and hovered while she got her bearings. 'Tom, go back into the theatre,' Beth ordered. 'I'm fine now and they'll need you.'

The orderly hesitated. 'David can help me,' Beth assured

him hastily. She wanted to talk to the student nurse about the earlier incident anyway.

Tom looked at David with a measured stare and Beth could tell he was trying to convey a don't-let-her-out-of-your-sight message to the younger man. Then he headed back toward the theatre. Beth wanted to remind the orderly she wasn't a child and she was the boss around here, but the nausea was growing and if she didn't eat soon she was seriously going to vomit.

David accompanied her to the tearoom and Beth indicated for him to take a chair as she grabbed a yoghurt from the fridge and devoured it. The trembling in her hands settled and the nausea stopped as if someone had flipped a switch. She sank back into the chair opposite David and closed her eyes gratefully.

What the hell was wrong with her? Was she coming down with something? Flu? She didn't feel feverish or have a sore throat or aching joints. Had she contracted some horrible virus with a long incubation period all those years ago when she'd lived overseas? She had worked in some fairly dodgy parts of the world.

This wouldn't do. Beth Rogers didn't get sick. In her eight years back at the General she hadn't had one sick day. And she certainly wasn't about to start now. Whatever it was it could just leave her alone. She didn't have time to be ill.

'Sister Rogers? Are you OK?'

Beth heard the slight crack in the younger man's voice and opened her eyes, pleased to find that the room was stable. She looked at the concern on his face. 'Yes, thanks, David,' she said, and smiled to allay his concerned look. 'I am now.'

'You gave us all a scare,' David said.

Beth noticed how his shoulders relaxed and the frown marring his forehead evened out. 'Don't worry, it won't happen again, I promise.'

The look of relief on David's face was almost comical and Beth suppressed a smile. 'What about you?' she asked. 'How are you doing? I hope you're not worried about contaminating the sterile package earlier.'

'No,' David sighed. 'I'm not...but...'

'But?' Beth could tell there was something bothering him.

'There's so much to learn, you know? I really like this specialty. But there's so many instruments and set-ups and procedures. I'm worried I'm going to stuff up all the time.'

Beth nodded, pleased that David was conscientious enough to care about his performance. It obviously wasn't just another rotation for him. She glimpsed a bit of her younger herself in him.

'Relax, David,' she said. 'We all make mistakes when we're first starting. And there is so much to learn. You know what I used to do? I used to spend every opportunity in the storeroom with the trays and an equipment manual, familarising myself with the different instruments. The basic ones and which combinations constituted which set-ups for which operations. I even used to come in on my days off. But I learned pretty quickly that way.'

'Yeah?'

David looked thoughtful and she could tell he was eager to learn. 'And don't forget. I'm here too. As well as the other senior staff. We're your resource people. Use us. OK?'

'OK,' he said, and smiled.

Beth smiled back, pleased with her rapport with the

student nurse and that he seemed so receptive to her advice. 'Now, get back to the theatre.'

Beth shut her eyes again after David had departed, her head lolling back against the wall. She wondered how long it would take the hospital grapevine to Chinese-whisper her little faint into something much more serious.

Beth lurched between feeling perfectly normal and desperately nauseated for the next few hours. Luckily she'd discovered that eating something was a very quick fix to the queasiness and an old packet of chocolate-coated sultanas she'd found in the bottom of her drawer worked miracles.

At one o'clock Rilla and Hailey arrived at her office. About the same time her stomach decided to become unsettled again and the sultanas were gone.

'We came as soon as we heard,' Hailey said, munching on a chocolate bar.

'Why are you still here?' Rilla added. 'You're obviously not well.'

Beth startled at their intrusion and looked up, spying her sister's chocolate bar. 'Quick, Hailey,' she said, standing and pointing, 'break me off a bit, will you?'

'This is my lunch,' Hailey complained.

'Hailey!' Beth practically snarled. 'I'm just asking for a bit. I'll buy you another one later. I need it now!'

Hailey blinked at the savageness of her sister's tone and snapped a bit off, handing it over. Rilla and her exchanged looks as their normally reserved, placid sister did a pretty good impression of the Cookie Monster.

'You OK, Beth?' Rilla asked.

'Sorry.' Beth grimaced, sinking into her chair. 'I've been

close to throwing up all morning and food's the only thing that helps.'

'So you've been feeling nauseated,' Rilla said as she sat in her usual chair, 'and you fainted this morning.'

Beth looked at both her sisters. 'Hell, you heard about that already?' She looked at her watch. Three hours. Even for the General that was fast.

'Well, actually, I heard that you'd had a seizure.' Hailey shrugged, sitting down as well, 'But Rilla assured me it was only a faint.'

'Exactly.' Beth nodded. 'Just a little faint. I think I'm coming down with a virus or something.'

'But you're never sick,' Hailey snorted.

'Maybe I'm a little rundown. I've been really tired the last few days. I'll be fine after a good night's sleep.'

A knock at her door interrupted the conversation and three sets of eyes turned to greet Gabe as he appeared in the doorway.

He exchanged pleasantries with Rilla and Hailey and then frowned at Beth. 'I didn't expect to see you still here. You should have gone home.'

'That's what I said,' Rilla said.

Beth ignored them both. 'You finished the list OK?'

Gabe nodded. 'Are you all right?'

'I'm fine,' she assured him testily. Everyone in Theatres, it seemed, had 'popped in' to check on her and she was getting heartily sick of it.

'Hey.' Gabe laughed, holding up his hands. 'Just asking. If you're going to make a habit of fainting in my theatre, I'd like to be forewarned.'

Beth shot him a thunderous look. She was feeling woozy

again which made her cranky. 'Fainting once in thirty-eight years is not a habit,' she snapped. 'Was there anything else?'

Gabe backed out of the doorway, his eyebrows raised at Beth's sisters.

'What?' Beth demanded moments later as her sisters fixed her with puzzled stares.

'Are you sure you're OK, Beth?' Rilla asked.

Beth sighed. 'Yes,' she said wearily, staving off more nausea. 'I'm just tired and light-headed and feel like throwing up all the time. I don't know what's wrong with me.'

'Well, if it was anyone but you and your non-existent sex life, I'd tell them to do a pregnancy test,' Hailey said. 'You have all the classic symptoms.'

Beth blinked and stared at Hailey open-mouthed. And then she laughed and her sisters joined her. That was completely preposterous!

The next morning, though, as Beth heaved into the toilet, the notion didn't seem so out there. Her period was late. Nothing out of the ordinary for her. She'd always had an erratic cycle. Anything up to seven weeks wasn't unusual for her. She'd been on the Pill to regulate it for years but she'd stopped taking it a while ago, wanting to give her body a break, and hadn't bothered to go back on it.

But it couldn't be possible. She and Gabe had used condoms. Yes, they weren't one hundred per cent infallible but they were pretty damn close. Had there been a faulty one that neither of them had noticed? Surely not. She was thirty-eight, for crying out loud—she should be practically infertile at her age.

Still, a tiny worm of excitement burrowed into her heart as she drove to work. The thought that she might be carrying a baby was overwhelming. The thing she'd wanted most since she'd been fifteen and her baby boy had been taken from her. Pregnant? A second chance? A baby to fill her arms and her life? Was she going to finally get a chance at being a mother?

The nausea haunted her throughout the day and she snacked constantly to keep it at bay. The worm of excitement burrowed deeper as she hugged the possible pregnancy to herself. She tried really hard not to get carried away but it occupied her every thought.

She shouldn't be excited. She knew that. When it turned out to be just a virus, she'd feel like a right idiot. And at her age, with no partner, set in her ways and a fantastic career, a baby should be a horrifying thought. Heaven alone knew what people would say. The hospital grapevine would be rife with rumours and speculation.

And then there was Gabe. She'd learnt enough about him to know that a baby would be an inconvenience to his career plans, as he had been an inconvenience to his father's. That he had a bright future which did not involve a family. She doubted very much whether he would welcome the idea of being a father.

But she knew one thing for sure. If she was pregnant she didn't need Gabe and she didn't give a fig for who thought what about her. She could do it without him. She was mature and financially secure—two things she hadn't been twenty-three years ago. And she was damned if she'd squander a second chance at being a mother.

Beth stopped in at a pharmacy on her way home that night and bought a home pregnancy test kit. She couldn't stand the speculation any longer. She had to know one way or the other.

She dumped her bag on the dining-room table and headed straight for the bathroom, brown chemist packet in hand. One minute later two pink stripes appeared before her eyes.

Two. Pink. Stripes.

Beth stared at the stick in disbelief. She shut her eyes and opened them again.

Two. Pink. Stripes.

She picked the test strip up and sat on the edge of the bath, looking at it. Her heart swelled with an emotion so overwhelming she felt tears prick her eyes. She smiled and then she laughed as tears brimmed and then fell down her cheeks. She wiped at them as she grinned like an idiot at the stick. She was pregnant. She really was pregnant.

'Hi, there, little guy,' she said, looking down at her flat stomach, cradling it with her hand.

Beth stood and looked at herself in the mirror. She wiped at her red eyes and blotchy face then turned to one side and smoothed her shirt over her abdomen. She took a deep breath and pushed her stomach out as far as it would go. She admired the artificial bump, swinging slightly from side to side to inspect the look from all angles.

She remembered doing the same thing twenty-three years ago. Although she had only been fifteen, she'd been in awe of the changes to her body and had loved how her belly had burgeoned as her baby had grown. She had known she wasn't supposed to be happy about the pregnancy, she certainly hadn't been allowed to want it, but she had loved the little life growing inside her so completely that secretly she'd welcomed every change to her body.

Thoughts of that time put a dampener on her rising joy. The air left her lungs and her stomach returned to its usual flatness. A seed of doubt sprouted roots. Her father's ugly words reverberated through her head. *Easy,* he had called her. *A slut. Irresponsible.* He'd told her repeatedly she'd be *a terrible mother.*

All the taunts and insults that at fifteen had crushed her spirit stirred inside her now. They still burned. As much now as they had back then. Simmered in her stomach like a boiling cauldron. What would her father say now? she wondered. That she hadn't changed? That she hadn't learned anything? Still knocked up and alone?

She looked at herself in the mirror. She looked pale, her red-rimmed blue eyes worried, her father's old ugly words furrowing her brow. She stared hard at her face as the chill of ancient insults battled with the evidence of her eyes. There were things in the mirror that hadn't been there all that time ago. She was older, stronger, confident.

OK, things weren't ideal. But she knew with sudden clarity that her father had been wrong. She would have been a damn good mother. As her body pulsed with the life of another, she knew it with absolute certainty. It would have been tough, sure. But she'd have managed because nothing would have been more important to her than her child. Just as this child was already her number-one priority.

'I'm sorry,' she whispered to her reflection apologising to the child she had never known.

She looked down at her stomach and splayed her hand across it. 'I promise,' she whispered. 'I promise to be the best mother that ever existed. I promise.'

She sat back on the edge of the bath again, her brain

buzzing. So, what now? The urge to tell Rilla and Hailey was amazingly intense. They were her sisters. They may not have been blood relatives but they were sisters in every way that counted and they'd been through too much together to lock them out of such a momentous occasion in her life.

But she knew she couldn't tell them before she told Gabe. And, frankly, she had no idea how she was going to do that. Or how he was going to react when she did.

Her sensible side was urging caution. She was, what? Beth performed a few calculations in her head—about six weeks gone. Realistically, one in four pregnancies ended in miscarriages, the odds worsening the older the mother, so at thirty-eight she was at an increased risk of losing the baby anyway.

The thought caused a physical pain in her chest and she clutched at her stomach. *Please, don't let me lose this baby too.* Beth already knew she'd trade her soul to keep this baby safe.

But telling people, making it public knowledge, seemed pointless until the highest risk period, the first trimester, had passed. Which gave her about six weeks. Six weeks to figure out what she was going to say to Gabe.

And in the interim it would be her little secret. She stood again and hugged her arms around her belly, giving her reflection a furtive smile.

She was having a baby. And no one could take that from her this time. No one.

CHAPTER FIVE

BETH sat in the case conference six weeks later, her hand on her belly, her gaze fixed on the sleeping faces of Brooke and Bridie. She'd just passed the milestone of her first trimester, the morning sickness had settled and she had actually allowed herself to believe that in six months' time she'd be holding her own baby in her arms.

Gabe was chatting with June and Scott and Erica Hamel, the plastic surgeon, about post-separation procedures to close the large residual defects at the back of the twins' heads. She was taking notes for future resource planning but the sweet smell of soap and baby powder kept wafting her way, distracting her.

Gabe's voice was also sidetracking her attention. Their night together two months ago still featured regularly in her dreams but had virtually faded from her head in their day-to-day dealings. Occasionally, though, she was caught unawares and his voice would hit a memory switch and she was back between the sheets with him.

She shut her eyes for a moment to dispel the fleeting but nonetheless entrancing image. June caught her eye and smiled at her. Beth blushed and smiled back. June gave her a saucy wink and Beth paled. Could June read minds? She sat up straighter and returned her attention to her notes and the conversation.

The Fishers left after their usual half-hour and Beth departed also. She was needed to scrub in this morning and she'd spared all the time she could.

'Were you OK in there?' June asked as they waited for the lift. 'You looked kind of daydreamy. Like you had a secret or something.'

Beth blushed again, her hand automatically falling to her stomach. She noticed June's speculative gaze and the urge to share was amazing. They'd got to know each other reasonably well over the weeks and Beth was so happy she wanted the world to know. She had come so close to telling Rilla and Hailey. But she knew she owed Gabe the news first.

'Not that I can blame you for looking a little glazed. Those conversations go right over my head.'

Beth laughed. 'I told you to butt in if you didn't understand anything,' she chided.

'That would make the meetings twice as long.' Scott joked. 'It's OK—we understand the basics. Our girls are in the best of hands. That's all that matters. We have faith in Gabe.'

Beth nodded. They all did. As a neurosurgeon about to separate conjoined twins, there wasn't anyone better. He was definitely *the* man. Beth just wished she could be so sure about his reaction to her pregnancy.

Another week passed, another Monday case conference, and Beth knew it was time. She couldn't put it off any longer. The coward in her wanted to put it off for ever. After all, he didn't have to know. She could probably keep the pregnancy disguised until after he'd left to go back home. But deep down she knew that wasn't fair.

Her baby was Gabe's baby also. And it was his right to know. Keeping it from him would be wrong. She didn't want or expect anything from him. He'd already told her that his career was his priority and that a family wasn't on his agenda. She just had to know that at the end of the day she'd been upfront.

Beth was dealing with the backlog of paperwork that inevitably came with the job. Not that she was actually taking much of it in—her internal dialogue was working overtime, building up the courage to seek Gabe out.

He was working back too, in Theatre Ten, getting in some more practice. At seven o'clock Beth could bear it no longer. *Just get it over with.* She threw her pen on her desk in disgust and marched towards the end of the corridor. Her entire body rocked to the hammering pulse coursing through her veins.

On her way past the storeroom she noticed some movement and stopped abruptly. All the theatres were finished for the day and the cleaning complete. 'Is someone in there?' she demanded at the open doorway.

David poked his head out from behind a shelf. 'It's just me,' he announced.

Beth relaxed. 'Cramming again?' She smiled. After her suggestion, David had practically haunted the storeroom in his spare time. He'd also called in at her office often to clarify things and Beth was impressed by the young man's dedication.

'Big case tomorrow?' she asked, joining him in the space between the shelves

'I'm scrubbing in with Dr Fallon tomorrow. My first neuro case.' He grimaced. 'I'm just going over the instruments.'

Beth gave him an admiring nod. It was nice to see a student nurse take his work so seriously. 'Gabe's a good teacher,' she said. 'You'll learn a lot.'

'I thought my ears were burning.'

Gabe's voice carried towards them and Beth's heart banged loudly against her ribs as she stuck her head out, as David had done earlier. One thing about working in Theatres was that you rarely heard people approach. The bootees that were worn over shoes muffled everyone's footsteps.

'You know what they say about eavesdroppers,' Beth chided, striving for a normal tone in her voice.

Gabe smiled at her and greeted David. 'I see you're scrubbing in with Kerry tomorrow on my morning list?' he said to the student nurse.

David nodded and Gabe noticed the nervous bob of his Adam's apple and the way the younger man constantly sought Beth's gaze. 'I look forward to it,' Gabe said as he brushed past them, looking for some more artery clamps. 'Be sure to ask me any questions.'

Gabe located a packet of clamps and departed, whistling as he went. Beth watched him leave, filling out his scrubs better than any man had a right to, and realised belatedly that she'd been on her way to talk to him. She excused herself from David, her pulse accelerating, knowing if she didn't do it tonight she might never get round to doing it.

She stood outside the swing doors and watched Gabe through the glass panel for a moment. He was behind the operating table, bent over the silicone 3-D model of the girls' fused craniums. Even through the panic that was twisting her stomach into knots she could see his dedication to Bridie and Brooke was absolute.

She took a deep breath and pushed through the door. He glanced up at her and then returned his attention to the vessel dissection he was working on.

'You must know that off by heart,' Beth said.

'Just about.' He grimaced, not looking up from the task. 'That's the purpose. As my father would have said, failure is not an option.'

Beth felt a stab of worry in her thundering heart. Everyone knew Gabe was expecting the operation to be a success but what if it wasn't? How would he react?

'Don't put too much pressure on yourself, Gabe. Everyone knows, including June and Scott that the girls are up against it.'

Gabe stopped what he was doing and glanced up at Beth. 'I know. But, hey, third time lucky, right?' He grinned and raised his crossed fingers.

Beth grinned back, feeling more relaxed now, and crossed her fingers also.

'So,' Gabe said casually, returning his attention to the model, 'David seems to have a little crush on you.'

Beth blinked. And then blushed. She hadn't been expecting that. 'What? Don't be ridiculous.'

Gabe smiled. '"Methinks the lady doth protest too much."'

'That's crazy,' Beth said ignoring his quote. 'I'm old enough to be his mother.' Beth faltered. *Wasn't that the truth?* 'I'm a mentor figure to him, that's all.'

Gabe laughed this time and Beth shot him a withering look. She'd come in here to announce his impending fatherhood and instead they were having a bizarre conversation about a non-existent workplace crush.

'Relax, Beth. I'm teasing.'

She glared at him furiously. 'Well, don't.'

Gabe curbed his smile and tried to look chastised. He'd noticed how often David sought Beth out and didn't think he was too far off the mark. There was certainly more than collegial feelings there on David's behalf. He remembered the crush he'd had as a med student on his first mentor, a professor of oncology. Older, powerful women had always done it for him. *Hell, he'd slept with Beth!*

Gabe returned to his work, a smile still playing at the corners of his mouth, expecting Beth to leave. When she hadn't moved a few minutes later and the weight of her stare was ruining his concentration he put the forceps down. 'Was there something you wanted?'

Beth took a deep breath. His crush allegation had thrown her but, damn it, this had to be done and he'd just given her as good an opening as any.

'I have to tell you something. It's…kind of…big. I want you to promise me you'll hear me out first before you say anything. OK?'

Gabe looked at her. She was twisting her hands in front of her and her voice sounded a little high. 'OK.'

OK. OK. She took another deep breath as the words she'd practiced deserted her. 'I don't really know how to say this.'

Gabe came around the front of the table. Beth looked two shades paler than a moment ago. *This was big.* He put his hands on his hips. 'Beth, you're worrying me now. I don't care how you say it. Just say it.'

Beth nodded. Then swallowed. 'I'm…' Her voice quavered and she cleared her throat. 'I'm pregnant.'

Gabe felt the words fall heavily, like stones, between them. Boulders. He didn't move. He didn't blink. He just stood and stared.

'I'm sorry. I know this wasn't in your plans. It wasn't in mine either. But it's happened. I know it's not what you want. That's fine. I don't want anything from you. I don't expect you to be involved in any way, shape or form. I just thought you should know.'

Beth finished and waited for a response. Gabe was staring at her, unmoving. Like the news had turned him into a statue. He didn't even blink. She couldn't tell if he was angry, upset or…having an absent seizure.

Gabe felt as if he was having an out-of-body experience. Like he'd wake up any moment and be in his bed at the hotel. He didn't feel anything. His mind, his thoughts, his body seemed…frozen.

'Gabe?'

He blinked at the sound of her voice but still his brain was blank.

'Gabe?' Beth prodded again. He was looking at her with an unfathomable expression and she placed a hand on her stomach.

His gaze flicked down to where her hand spanned her flat belly. His child was inside her? He shook his head. 'But…but we used protection.'

Beth heard the disbelief in his voice and could see the comical aspect despite the seriousness. A doctor, a *neurosurgeon* standing there, trying to tell her that condoms were infallible?

'Yes, we did.'

It took a few more moments for Gabe to process the information. 'And you're sure?'

She nodded. 'I'm thirteen weeks.'

Thirteen weeks? Gabe leant back against the table. 'You've known for a while,' he stated, still stunned.

Beth shrugged. 'I didn't see the point in turning your world upside down until I'd carried the baby through the first trimester.'

He nodded. *Made sense.* Gabe rubbed the back of his neck. A kid? He didn't have time for a kid. 'I...I don't know what to say.'

Gabe looked totally horrified. His green eyes were dazed as he stroked his jaw absently. 'It was a shock for me also,' Beth said quietly. Part of her had hoped for a different reaction but deep down she'd known the news wouldn't be welcome.

He looked into her steady blue gaze, her hand still cradling her stomach. It may have been a shock but she seemed quite together about it. Granted, she'd had longer than him to get used to it but she didn't seem panicked or stricken or upset. Surely at thirty-eight this must have been a most unwelcome development?

'So...you want to...have the baby?'

Beth took an involuntary step back, her hands tightening protectively around her stomach. 'More than I've ever wanted anything.'

Gabe stared at her. Her tone brooked no argument, her mouth a tight line. 'But...what about...' He groped around for something to say while his brain tried to make sense of the situation. 'What about your career?'

'My career, Gabe? Or your career?' she asked icily.

Gabe shook his head to clear it. His mind was a jumble. 'I'm sorry...I'm making a bit of a hash of this... I just assumed that as you were single with no kids by now, it was through choice...that children weren't on your agenda.'

Beth felt a well of emotion stronger than her anger rise in her chest and tears pricked her eyes. How many nights had she cried herself to sleep because her arms had ached so much? 'No. It wasn't through choice. It was just the way it panned out.'

Gabe couldn't believe the conversation they were having. To think ten minutes ago, separating conjoined twins had been his biggest worry. It seemed like a walk in the park compared to this.

'You really want to do this...don't you?'

Beth heard the disbelief in his voice. It was obvious he thought being lumbered with a baby was a fate worse than death. She had to make him see that she wanted this baby desperately. That it wasn't some last whim of an almost barren nearly-forty female.

'Twenty-three years ago I had a baby. A little boy. I was fifteen. I gave him up for adoption. It broke my heart.' Beth's voice cracked at the effort it took to suppress the memories of that time and not break down in front of him. 'So, yes, Gabe,' she continued, her voice trembling with the fierceness needed to protect the baby growing inside her. 'I do. I do want to have the baby.'

Gabe stared at Beth, her second shocking revelation in as many minutes hanging between them. It was even harder to absorb than the first one had been. *She'd had a baby?* This was the chunk of information he'd sensed she'd left out that first day at Barney's. It was obviously the reason why she'd run away and why she'd ended up fostered by the Winterses.

Gabe pushed away from the table to pace, feeling like his head was about to explode. *What the hell was he going to do?* He paced for a few minutes, conscious of Beth watching him. He turned and looked at her, one hand on her stomach, the other clenched into a fist by her side.

It was obvious her mind was made up. And given what he now knew, he could understand why. But still...

He lived on the other side of the world. His private practice, his entire career was ten of thousands of kilometres away. A twenty-four-hour trip by plane. Oh, God, did she expect him to propose? Would she even come to the UK?

'Well, of course...I'll...' he swallowed '...support you in anything you want to do.'

Beth shook her head, taking pity on him. She'd just dumped an awful lot of information in his lap. 'No, Gabe. I told you. I don't want you to. And I certainly don't expect you to. I know this isn't what you want. I'm perfectly happy to raise this child alone. Just go back to England when your contract runs out and forget about us. I won't blame you or think any less of you.'

Gabe stopped pacing. He searched her face. He couldn't believe she was being so calm. Giving him an out. She hadn't insisted on a gold band and a white picket fence. In fact, she'd absolved him from all responsibility. Wasn't she supposed to want that? This was too much. It was all too much.

'You really mean that, don't you? You'd raise this baby on your own.'

Beth frowned. 'Of course.'

Gabe reeled. This was madness. 'Doesn't that scare you witless? Isn't that just too…daunting?'

Beth nodded. 'Of course it's scary and daunting and overwhelming and there are a lot of voices in my head, from my past…my father, my stepmother…that make me doubt myself. But I'm not fifteen this time around and I have a supportive family and a home and a stable income. And I want this more than anything.'

'I don't know what to say.' He rubbed the back of his neck again. 'I don't know what to think.'

'Of course,' she replied. 'I've just dumped this in your lap and I'm sorry, you've got enough to worry about, I realise. You need to concentrate on Brooke and Bridie. Don't worry about me. Or the baby.'

She was seriously going to let him walk away?

Gabe knew he didn't want to be a father. He hadn't planned it and he hadn't asked for it. The question was, could he just fly back to the UK and turn his back on his child? Have nothing to do with it? Ever? What kind of a human being did that make him?

Harlon Fallon's son.

He shivered. Even if Beth was as OK with it as she appeared, it just didn't seem right. Didn't his baby deserve two parents? A father as well? One that was around. Interested? Involved? Didn't he want to spare his child the insecurities that had plagued him because of his absent father?

How many nights had he gone to bed with a churned-up stomach knowing that he had a father out there that would rather be in a hospital full of sick people than at home with him? How often had he questioned his identity and his way in life with no father figure as a guide? How miserable had he felt when no matter how hard he had tried to get his father's attention, nothing had ever seemed to work? He'd had to become a doctor before Harlon Fallon had taken any notice of him.

When he looked back at his childhood he could describe it in one word. Incomplete. Could he inflict that on another child? His own child?

'I want to help.'

Beth blinked. 'Wh-what?'

Gabe blinked too, not sure he'd actually said the words. 'This baby...it's my responsibility too.'

Beth felt her pulse slow right down, her blood roar in her ears. He wanted to help? His responsibility? What did that mean? She took a step back. 'I don't understand. I didn't think you'd want to... It's OK, you can walk away, Gabe. I won't judge you. I'm perfectly capable of taking care of this baby. I own my own home, I have good savings, a few investments and a well-paid job. We'll be okay.'

The more determined she seemed to push him away, the more certain he became. It obviously hadn't occurred to her that he'd want any part of it. And, frankly, it scared the hell out of him but as each second ticked by his convictions crystallised.

'I'm not walking. I'm not sure I understand why you're so determined to make me. We both had fathers that left a lot to be desired. They were absent. Emotionally distant. I'm not going to make the same mistake with my own kid. Don't you want better for our child?'

Beth looked at him still dumbfounded by his desire to be involved. 'Of course. I just didn't think you'd want to be involved. I don't want you to feel you have to be out of some stupid sense of propriety or duty.'

'I'm the father,' Gabe said testily. 'It *is* my duty.'

'You know what I mean,' Beth said, her voice tinged with exasperation. 'How do you think it's going to work? Your career is taking off. I can't go to the UK, Gabe.'

Was that what he wanted? Hell, he didn't know. He needed to think things through. All he knew was that he wanted to be part of his child's life. He wanted to be more than a sperm donor and a mysterious gift every birthday.

Gabe shrugged, buying time for his startled thought processes to compute the information. 'Why not?'

Beth felt a knot of tension pull hard in her stomach. 'I can't leave… I have to stay. My son…he may try and get in contact with me one day. I need to be here for that…in case.'

Gabe leant heavily against the operating table. Beth's twenty-three-year-old son. Another angle to consider. Beth had had weeks to think this through, look at it in minute detail. The shocking news had rendered him completely incapable of anything other than breathing, and yet she had everything planned out.

'I don't know, Beth. I don't know how it'll work. All I know is that I want to be involved. I need time to think about this.'

Beth heard the weary note in his voice, still surprised at his insistence. Shocked, actually. Shocked was a much better word. He hadn't been in any of the plans she'd weaved over the last six weeks. And she wasn't entirely sure she wanted to make room for him. She'd been so sure he'd run. A tremor of apprehension ran through her as she glanced at him uneasily. What did that mean for her future now?

'Of course, Gabe,' Beth said, pulling her straying thoughts back into line. 'There's a lot to take in. And your plate was pretty full to begin with. We don't have to make any concrete decisions at the moment. Nothing has to be decided for ages yet. Let's just get the separation out of the way first.'

Time. They both needed time to think. Adjust.

Gabe leant against the table again, admiring her ability to prioritise calmly. All his focus and energies since arriving in Brisbane had been concentrated on the twins. Every waking moment, even some sleeping ones and certainly every spare minute had been given to the operation. Yet this piece of news had completely obliterated Brooke and Bridie from his mind.

She was right, though—first things first. And the Fisher twins took that honour. He nodded. 'Separation first.'

'I'll let you get on with your practice,' Beth said, backing away.

'Sure,' Gabe said absently. He looked down at the discarded silicone model and knew there was no way he was going to be able to concentrate on that tonight.

Beth reached the door and paused. She looked over her shoulder at a bewildered Gabe who was staring unseeingly at the practice model. He looked like he'd had the stuffing knocked out of him. Maybe she should have kept quiet?

'I'm sorry,' she said. 'I thought you'd want to know.'

Gabe looked up. 'Of course,' he sighed. 'You did the right thing.'

He watched her open the door. It seemed odd that they were parting like this after such news. Finding out their night together had created a life was about as intimate as you could get. An embrace seemed more appropriate.

'When's the baby due?' Gabe called after her.

Beth paused. 'September thirty,' she said, and went on her way, letting the door swing shut behind her.

The silence in Theatre Ten was deafening as a barrage of conflicting thoughts stampeded through Gabe's head. Six months. *Hell.*

A month passed. Beth and Gabe were kept busy with their normal workload as well as the preparations for the separation. Things were initially a little awkward between them again but with their busy schedules and tacit agreement to focus on the twins, their professionalism came to the fore.

Their relationship continued to be that of colleagues. Mutual respect and consideration. In fact, at times it even bordered on friendship. But apart from the odd query after her health, Gabe didn't refer to the pregnancy and there'd been no further discussion about the baby as preparations for the separation ramped up.

But one month shy of the scheduled operation Beth was woken at three in the morning by Gabe's delicious accent. It was brisk and businesslike. No late-night lovers' chat like the last time they'd spoken at this hour of the morning.

'Brooke and Bridie have been admitted to the intensive care unit. Bridie had a prolonged seizure.'

Beth struggled through the layers of sleep, her heart pounding, and not just because of the unexpected turn of events. 'Are we going in?'

'Not yet. I'll keep you posted.'

Beth stared at the dead phone for a few seconds before placing it back on its cradle. She fell back against the pillows, her brain kicking into overdrive, her heart beating crazily. Were they ready for this? Had they practised enough?

She placed a hand over her belly where Gabe's baby was growing safe and well, knowing she'd slay a dragon for their unborn baby. She thought about June and Scott and suppressed the urge to get out of bed and rush to ICU to be with them. They had a very supportive family and Beth knew they'd be rallying around.

Oddly enough, she wanted to go to Gabe more. She knew how much he'd invested in this operation and how much pressure he was under to make it a third successful separation. She'd also seen how close he'd become to the Fishers, as they all had, and knew he'd be taking this development hard.

But, father of her child or not, they didn't have that kind of relationship. In fact, they had gone to pains to maintain a professional distance and she wouldn't ruin that by tearing up to the hospital in the middle of the night to hold his hand. She would see him tomorrow and in the meantime she'd go back to sleep.

Hopefully.

The next few days were fraught for the Fisher twins. Bridie was loaded with anti-convulsants but because the girls shared a blood supply through the intricate meshing of cranial vessels, that complicated things for Brooke.

Bridie went on to develop a pleural effusion and started to show signs of renal and liver impairment. Her blood pressure needed drugs to support it, a tricky balance for ICU doctors who had to consider the effects on both girls.

Gabe was worried that Bridie might not make it, that she would die before separation, flooding her sister's body with toxins that would give Brooke mere hours to live. With Bridie's heart not the strongest, Gabe was reluctant to subject the smaller twin to the rigours of prolonged neurosurgery but he knew they were walking a fine line.

Beth visited regularly. It didn't seem to matter what time she popped in, Gabe was always there. Standing with Scott and June, talking to the ICU doctors or consulting with other specialists. He was upbeat with the Fishers but she could tell he was tense and gravely concerned.

Two days later, Bridie's condition worsened again, with the development of more seizures, and a joint decision was made to go ahead with the op. Gabe knew their hand was being forced but that was just the way it happened sometimes and no matter how much he would have liked both twins to be in optimum shape, life had thrown them a curve ball. He had to operate now or risk losing both of them.

He rang Beth again in the wee small hours. 'We're going in. How soon can we get the team assembled?'

Beth heard the slight huskiness in his voice and knew that Gabe wasn't thrilled about the circumstances. She rubbed the lingering traces of sleep from her eyes her brain racing ahead. 'A few hours.'

'See you then.'

CHAPTER SIX

IT WAS barely seven on Saturday morning as the team members required for the beginning of the operation assembled in Theatre Ten, waiting for the twins to arrive. Half of them had blue scrub tops and gowns, the other half green. Bridie's team wore blue, Brooke's green. They waited silently, rehearsing the steps in their head that they'd honed over the last few months.

The ten-strong anaesthetic team, led by Don Anderson talked quietly, going over their strategies to manage vital signs and minimise blood loss and the logistics of moving the babies once the separation was complete.

Beth scrubbed in, along with several other nurses, and oversaw the set-ups. Circulating nurses opened the mountains of sterile equipment that would be needed, passing them to the scrub nurses, who organised their trolleys methodically. She was hyper-aware of Gabe standing with the other scrubbed surgeons huddled around the numerous images, going over their last-minute plans.

Shortly she would take her place beside him for who knew how many hours. They both wore blue. It had been decided from the beginning that, given his experience, that

Gabe would take the more fragile twin on their separation. And this morning he had insisted she be at his side.

'I want the best neuro scrub nurse on my team,' he'd said. 'Bridie has an uphill battle. More than her sister. I need the best to give her any hope.'

And so now she was wearing blue and hoping, as were they all, she didn't let him down. Gabe turned and looked directly at her.

'Are we ready, Beth?'

Beth looked around at the team and took in their silent nods. 'As ready as we'll ever be.'

The anaesthetised twins were rolled into the theatre. For a few seconds all movement and all conversation ceased. This was what it was about. Two fragile babies, dwarfed by the complex equipment surrounding them and lost in a sea of blue and green strangers who held their fate in their hands.

'Let's get this show on the road,' Gabe announced, and the team kicked into action.

Once plastic surgeons had made the first incision and exposed the area it was Gabe's turn. As he and fellow neurosurgeon Eve Mitchell worked, he could feel sweat building on his brow as his heart hammered madly in his chest. *So far, so good.*

They were about to perform the craniotomy that would open a window into the twins' brains. No 3-D computer image or plastic moulded replica. This was the moment they'd prepared and practised for. The moment of truth. The enormity was almost overwhelming.

'Wipe,' he said.

Beth grabbed one of the folded surgical sponges as

Gabe turned towards her, surprised that he required it already. They'd only been at it for a short while.

She glanced into his peridot eyes, piercingly intense above his mask, and thought she saw a fleeting second of uncertainty. *Poor Gabe.* Bridie's condition had just magnified the pressure on him. She gave him an encouraging smile, even though she knew he couldn't see it behind her mask.

Gabe saw it anyway, reflected in her blue gaze as he bent down slightly for her to mop his brow. Their gazes locked for a fleeting moment and the faith he saw there bolstered his confidence.

The procedure took hours as they slowly and cautiously worked their way through the spaghetti-sized blood vessels. Gabe stopped several times to consult the pre-op scans and diagrams held up for him by circulating nurses.

The anaesthetic team kept a close eye on the babies' vital signs. Gabe asked for regular updates, only too aware that any ongoing blood loss could be catastrophic to patients this size. Transfusions ran to replace the lost volume but it was a delicate balance. Too much could upset the girls' natural clotting factors.

Gabe checked the clock and was surprised to see six hours had passed. His neck and shoulders ached a little from being hunched over the small operating area and he knew it was time to take a break. He and Eve signalled their intention to hand over and allow two fresh surgeons to take their places.

During one of the many pre-op discussions it had been decided that six hours should be the maximum period any member of the team spent in the theatre at any one time unless there was an emergency or the surgery was at a critical stage. Six hours on, maximum. Two hours off, minimum.

Their replacements arrived and all the scrubbed staff, including nurses, degowned and headed for the staffroom for a well-earned break. The team members waiting in the staff room applauded as Gabe entered the room.

'Don't get too carried away,' Gabe warned.

Yes, things were going according to plan and he was cautiously optimistic, but he knew only too well that things could go pear-shaped very quickly. They had a lot of brain to get through still and Bridie's frailty worried him.

Beth, feeling slightly nauseated from lack of food, grabbed a bite to eat. Breakfast of tea and toast seemed an eon ago. Someone had brought in cream buns and she bit into one gratefully. There was a mixture of excitement and cautious optimism in the staffroom and she found it difficult not to be infected by it.

The wall-mounted monitors Beth had arranged previously relayed images and sound from the theatre, and as they chatted and relaxed they could keep an eye on the operation. Being able to watch the proceedings and discuss them was invaluable to keeping them all focused and up to date.

Several shift changes came and went from Theatre Ten. The day was long and night fell without anyone being aware of it. Operating theatres were a windowless world, insulated and artificial. History was being made at the General with each tiny slice of the scalpel and that was all anyone was aware of.

As the night wore on, slow progress was being made on teasing the two brains apart. The staffroom was littered with empty coffee-mugs, discarded food wrappings and staff catching some shut-eye in chairs, while others watched the screens with bleary eyes and murmured quietly among themselves.

Gabe and Beth were back in the thick of it, standing side by side. He was frustrated at the snail-pace progress and worried about the increased bleeding.

They placed special gauze soaked in anti-coagulant as they traveled deeper into the dissection to try and minimise the ooze, and anaesthetic nurses hung bag after bag of blood, platelets and fresh frozen plasma to enhance the twins' clotting factors. But Gabe knew that the longer it took, the worse shape the girls would be in by the end.

Frustratingly, as he meticulously separated the grey matter, the tissues would swell and push into each other again, making the going even more difficult.

Beth could sense Gabe's growing frustration with the un-cooperative brain tissue. He was tired, they all were. Neither of them had slept—too wired to relax. But at their next break she was going to insist. Despite the slowness, they were much closer to the end and the head of the team had to be alert.

An hour later the brain tissue began to bleed heavily. Gabe's fingers worked quickly, accepting instruments from Beth to stem the haemorrhage. Just then the monitor alarm went off.

'What is it?' Gabe asked, without looking away from his task.

'Bridie's pressure's dropping. She's bradycardic,' Don Anderson supplied.

It took thirty minutes to stabilise Bridie again. Luckily Brooke's vitals remained as steady as a rock.

Several hours later they degowned again. 'Get some shut-eye,' Beth ordered. She stopped by the blanket warmer and pulled a deliciously toasty blanket out. 'Go put your head on my desk.'

Gabe shook his head. 'I'll grab forty winks in the staffroom.'

'No,' Beth insisted. 'You won't. You'll sit and yack with fifteen different people about the procedure.' She pushed the blanket into his arms. 'If everything goes according to plan, the separation is imminent in the next few hours. The girls need you rested.'

'I'm fine,' he said abruptly.

'Dr Fallon!'

His head snapped up and their gazes locked. They'd stopped all that ridiculous formality weeks ago.

'You are not fine. Bridie needs the best. You are not at your best.'

Gabe saw the fire in her eyes and appreciated her frankness. She was right. But what about her? She was eighteen weeks pregnant after all.

'What about you, Beth?' He placed a hand against her stomach. 'You must be extra-tired. How are you holding up?'

Beth was surprised by his action. He hadn't mentioned the baby to her once in the last month. His hand there felt so good, so right, so intimate she had to suppress the urge to cover it with her own.

Gabe liked how it felt to touch her there. Operating on the twins made it impossible to ignore he would soon have a baby of his own. Already, despite his conflicting emotions, he felt a weird kind of connection to his child. It enabled him to put himself in Scott and June's shoes. To realise the operating area beneath his hands belonged to somebody's babies.

'I'm OK,' she said, moving away slightly, conscious that

anyone could come out of the staffroom and see them. They'd agreed to keep news of the pregnancy quiet until after the separation. 'I suspect I've had more sleep than you the last few nights.'

Gabe dropped his hand, feeling strangely bereft. God, he must be tired. He smiled grudgingly. 'Sleep has been rather elusive.' He'd been pulling long nights in the ICU. 'You'll wake me if—'

'I will get you immediately if anything happens.'

Gabe rubbed his jaw, a shadow of stubble evident. He gave her a slow, grateful smile. 'Thanks, Beth.'

Beth nodded as he brushed past her and she ignored the mad flutter in her chest. His acknowledgement of their baby had stirred something in her that she hadn't allowed herself to buy into. Gabe as a father figure. And she couldn't afford to buy into it now either.

Beth stood in the doorway to her office, a steaming mug of coffee and several pieces of honey toast on a plate in one hand. Gabe was slumped over her desk, his face relaxed in slumber, his stubble growth more pronounced. His theatre cap was still firmly in place and he'd bunched some of the blanket beneath his face to act as a pillow.

His full lips were parted slightly and she allowed herself the brief fantasy of waking him by placing her mouth on his. He really did have very tempting lips.

'Gabe,' she called quietly.

He didn't move. Beth walked in, placed the food and drink on the edge of her desk and moved closer to him.

'Gabe,' she whispered, and gave his shoulder a gentle shake.

Gabe was awake instantly, his head rising from the desk. 'I'm awake,' he announced loudly. His eyes came to focus on Beth's and he gave her a sleepy smile. 'What's happening?' He sat up fully alert now, pushing the blanket off his shoulders and stretching his neck from side to side.

Beth placed the coffee and toast in front of him. 'They think they're only a couple of hours away but the team is tiring.'

Gabe nodded. 'How long have I been asleep?'

'Nearly four hours.'

'Have the twins been stable?'

'Bridie's required some support for her blood pressure but she seems to be holding her own. Brooke's still soldiering on.'

Gabe took a sip of his coffee. 'OK. I'll eat this then go back in. Did you sleep?'

Beth nodded. 'A little.' He had a mark on his face from the weave of the cellular blanket and she smiled at the criss-cross pattern marring his cheek.

'What? Have I got drool on my chin?'

Beth grinned. 'No. Blanket face.'

Gabe laughed. 'Wait till you see my hat hair after thirty hours.'

Beth laughed too. 'You won't be alone there.' It felt good to laugh after the pressure of the last twenty-four hours and a couple of months of stilted formality.

Gabe offered her one of his pieces of toast. Despite having just had a piece, she took one. High-stakes surgery was not her forte and the baby was letting her know it didn't approve of the extra stress. A vague feeling of nausea had taken up permanent residence in her stomach and, as always, eating helped.

They munched quietly for a few moments. 'Looks like we did get to have breakfast together after all,' he said, and smiled at her. 'Not quite what I'd planned on. Room service at the hotel do the best omelettes and Danish pastries.'

Beth swallowed the toast, which suddenly felt dry and cardboard-like. 'Gabe.'

Gabe heard the note of warning and felt too weary to tease any further. 'I know. Sorry. Inappropriate. Forget I mentioned it.'

'Forgotten.' She straightened, giving her scrub top a firm yank. 'I'll see you at the sinks.'

Gabe sighed as she left, his appetite deserting him. Forgetting their night together, forgetting she was carrying his baby had been a lot easier when they hadn't been practically glued at the hip for the last twenty-four hours.

'Separation imminent,' Gabe announced, looking up into the camera above his head for the benefit of those in the staffroom. 'I need all hands on deck.'

His pulse picked up. In less than thirty minutes Bridie and Brooke would finally be separate and the surgical team that had been operating as one would become two.

The second table was wheeled in by orderlies and the wheels locked in place. More scrub and scout nurses appeared. They draped the new table in preparation to receive Brooke and continue the delicate process of closure. It had been decided that as Brooke was the more stable twin, she was the best candidate to be moved.

The anaesthetic team prepared for the transfer procedure, as they had practised. Brooke's surgeons stood scrubbed and ready to receive her. Kelly, Brooke's scrub nurse, counted instruments and sponges with the circulating nurses. The theatre was now crowded.

And then the moment came. The last bit of tissue and bone was excised and Brooke was gently lifted and slowly transferred across. The manoeuvre was textbook and the collective breaths of nearly thirty people were expelled in one audible exhalation.

But there was no time for self-congratulation as Brooke's team swarmed around the table and the surgeries continued.

'She's bleeding too much again,' Gabe said, his attention only on Bridie. 'How's her vitals?'

'Pressure dropping,' Don confirmed. 'She's getting more tachy. ECG changes.'

'Come on, Bridie,' Gabe pleaded quietly behind his mask. 'Stay with us.'

Beth and the other scrub nurse frantically passed instruments to Gabe and the two other surgeons who were trying valiantly to get the bleeding under control. The anaesthetic teamed push fluids and administered drugs to bolster Bridie's failing heart.

'She's going brady,' the anesthetic nurse announced.

'Come on, Bridie,' Gabe said, his fingers working desperately to control the bleeding.

Don and his team worked continuously to restore the failing twin's circulation, to no avail.

'Surgical staff step back from the table,' Don ordered, as Bridie's ECG displayed life-threatening bradycardia.

Beth and Gabe, along with the others, dropped their instruments frantically and stepped back, hands held slightly in front of them to protect their sterility. Bridie's full anaesthetic team converged on the table, taking turns at external chest compressions.

Fifteen minutes later Gabe moved closer to see what was happening. 'What's her rhythm like?'

The anesthetic nurse stopped compressions momentarily. The line on the monitor barely fluttered.

'It's no good,' Don said to Gabe. 'She's lost too much blood.'

Gabe shook his head. *No*. They hadn't just performed thirty hours of neurosurgery to give up after fifteen minutes.

'More adrenaline,' Gabe said, pushing into the circle surrounding tiny Bridie and taking over compressions.

Twenty minutes passed. Thirty. Forty-five. More drugs. More chest compressions. They even achieved a shockable rhythm at one stage and used the defibrillator twice. Beth stood behind Gabe, watching his erect frame, listening to his orders, her heart breaking for him. He'd invested so much in this operation.

Don's gaze caught hers and she knew what he was thinking. It was no use. Bridie had fought magnificently but it was over. The odds had been stacked against her and it was time to be let go.

But nobody wanted to contradict Gabe. He was the surgeon who had made it all possible, who had so very nearly succeeded, and he was well liked and respected. They all wanted to give Gabe and Bridie every chance. But it was past time.

Beth walked into the circle. 'Gabe,' she said in a low voice.

Gabe ignored her as he pumped at the tiny chest with his blood-covered gloves.

'Gabe,' she said, louder this time.

'More adrenaline,' Gabe said to Don.

The anaesthetist looked at Beth again. 'Dr Fallon…' he said.

'Damn it, Don. I said more adrenaline,' Gabe snapped. *Come on, Bridie, come on.*

'Gabe!' Beth used the voice she always used when dealing with recalcitrant staff. It wasn't loud, she didn't want to draw the attention of the whole theatre, but it had just the right note of don't-mess-with-me.

Gabe looked down at Beth, seeing her for the first time.

'It's time.' She placed her hands over his.

Gabe shook his head, his hands still moving, their gazes locked. *She was just a tiny baby.*

She nodded. 'She's had nearly an hour of downtime,' she said, knowing that even if by some miracle Bridie's heart was to suddenly start, there would no doubt be serious brain damage. 'You've done all you could.'

Gabe knew she was right. Knew she was making sense. But he'd promised June and Scott that he would do everything in his power to give them back two live, separated little girls. How could he break his promise?

'Let her go, Gabe,' Beth said gently staring into his conflicted green eyes. 'Bridie's telling you she's had enough. Her little body can't take any more.'

She was right. Gabe's hands stilled. Her body had been through a huge ordeal and her recent frailty had stacked the odds against her even further. He sighed and withdrew his hands.

He looked at the clock on the wall. 'Time of death fifteen twenty-five hours.'

He peeled off his gloves as the whole theatre fell silent.

Nobody moved for a moment or two as they took in Bridie's pale, lifeless body. She looked so small and de-fenceless among the green drapes.

Beth raised her hand to touch Gabe on the arm as a wave of sadness overwhelmed her. Everyone looked devastated and she knew Gabe would be feeling the worst of all of them. But she remembered herself at the last moment and dropped her hand to her belly instead grateful for the tiny fluttering movements she felt there.

Gabe roused himself like the true professional he was. This day wasn't over yet. He turned to the table behind him. 'How's Brooke?' he asked.

'We've achieved primary closure,' the plastic surgeon said.

'Vitals?' Gabe queried the anesthetist.

'Stable.'

He looked down at Brooke. Her head was wrapped in a turban-like head bundle. Her eyes were puffy and bruised-looking. Her tiny body was criss-crossed with a multitude of fluid lines and monitoring wires. A bag of blood was running with all the other fluids.

She looked pale, although not as pale as her sister. 'What's her haemoglobin?'

'Ninety.'

Gabe nodded, satisfied with the figure considering all that Brooke had been through and was still to endure. She was by no means out of the woods yet. 'Let's get her to ICU.'

He turned back to Bridie. Beth was assisting one of the plastics team, who was closing the gaping head wound amidst a flurry of clean-up activity. He stood beside her.

'Nearly done,' Beth said.

'Thanks,' Gabe said, admiring the surgeon's neat suturing.

Beth was hyper-aware of him beside her. Being intimate with him had given her a crash course in his body language and, getting to know him and his perfectionism in the last months, she guessed he was reliving those last moments, searching for something he could have done differently. Maybe wondering what his father would have done.

'Why don't you go and talk to Scott and June?' she suggested, knowing there was no use in second-guessing him.

She made a mental note to organise a series of team debriefs. Everyone involved had a huge emotional investment in the case. It would be a bond they'd share for ever. It was important to be able to discuss their reactions to the marathon surgery and the less than ideal outcome.

Gabe nodded, dreading the moment he would have to tell the Fishers that their precious little Bridie hadn't pulled through. It didn't matter that they'd been given a very guarded prognosis and this type of outcome had been discussed at length with them. One of their daughters was dead. No matter how prepared someone was for that, it would still rock them to the core.

CHAPTER SEVEN

THE clean-up was a mammoth task and Beth stayed to help out. The number of instrument trays alone they'd been through added up to the amount they'd normally use in one day for all ten theatres. She slipped into the dirty corridor and gave the staff there a hand before sitting at her desk and reworking the week's roster.

Several of the nursing staff involved in the Fisher case were due back on tomorrow morning and Beth stayed until she'd been able to give them two days off and still cover the roster. It involved ringing staff at home and begging favours and also organising agency cover but she managed it.

She had half expected Gabe to drop by and was absurdly disappointed when he didn't. She was worried about him and needed to reassure herself that he was OK. She decided to drop into the PICU on her way to Barney's for the team get-together, guessing correctly that Gabe would be there.

Brooke was in a side room and her nurse brushed past Beth as she approached, leaving Gabe alone in the room with the surviving twin. Scott and June were absent. Beth stood silently in the doorway, watching Gabe talk quietly to Brooke.

'I'm sorry,' he whispered, stroking the fingers of her tiny

pale hand encumbered by an arterial line. 'I tried, we all did...but your sister was...very weak. She's always going to be with you, though. In here.' Gabe lightly tapped Brooke's chest, expertly avoiding the wires that snaked haphazardly across her tiny body that could trigger an alarm.

Beth backed away, tears in her eyes. The crack in his voice was heartbreaking and it wasn't right to intrude on his private vigil. Her thoughts were jumbled and she knew it was a dangerous moment. A moment when she could have crazy fantasies of love and white picket fences. Beth knew thoughts such as those shouldn't be given any credence at times like this so she quashed them ruthlessly as she left the ICU and walked quickly away.

The sun was setting as she walked across the road to Barney's. The team was meeting for a quick meal and a casual debrief, and Beth knew it was vital to support her staff in this area. All her nurses had been affected by Bridie's death and she knew it was important to lead by example and attend these all important sessions, be they casual or formal.

The mood was subdued. There was satisfaction and immense pride that Brooke had made it but it was over-shadowed by Bridie's death. To Beth's surprise, Gabe wasn't there, and she suspected that this contributed to the general gloom.

Gabe had been the leader and his positivity and enthusiasm had buoyed them all whenever the task had seemed too overwhelming. Now that things hadn't gone according to plan, everyone was looking for some reassurance that they hadn't let him down.

Beth's feelings see-sawed from her earlier tenderness to

plain annoyed. And every time the pub door opened and everyone's heads swiveled, looking for Gabe, she got crankier. His no-show had been inconsiderate of the team's needs. The team that had worked their butts off beside him. That were as emotionally invested in the Fisher case as he had been. His absence had left them rudderless.

The group broke up early. Everyone was tired after the marathon surgery and the loss of Bridie had put a dampener on their spirits. Beth imagined that had both twins pulled through, they would have partied late into the night, despite their exhaustion. The gathering felt anti-climatic rather than a celebration of an amazing feat.

Beth headed straight for Gabe's hotel, her irritation having increased as she'd watched her colleagues leave Barney's, their shoulders slumped. He couldn't build them up and then desert them when his grand vision had failed. He'd known the odds had been long from the beginning, and he should have been at Barney's with them, commiserating and assuring them that everyone had done all they'd been able to.

She had a brief thought as she rapped on his door that he might not even be at the hotel, but that was soon proved wrong when he opened the door. Shirtless.

Gabe stared at her. 'You're not room service.'

Beth stared back, her gaze dragged downwards to his magnificently bare chest. 'No.'

He stood aside. 'Do you want to come in?'

With you half-naked? But considering she'd come to give him a piece of her mind, she thought it better to do it in the privacy of his room. She walked through his doorway, taking special care not to brush against him.

'Do you want a drink?' he asked, staring at her very erect back.

'No,' she said abruptly, angrier now that her thoughts had been scattered by the sight of his beautifully hard chest.

Gabe shrugged. 'I'm getting some chips from room service. I can order extra if you like.'

Beth turned. 'I've eaten. At Barney's. With everyone else.'

Gabe saw the accusation glitter in her blue eyes. 'Yeah, sorry about that. I was wrecked.'

He did look exhausted. The shadow of stubble that had been growing at his jaw was more pronounced now. His caramel hair was rumpled. Beth folded her arms across her chest and hardened her heart. 'We were all wrecked.'

Gabe heard the steel in her reply. He took a moment to look at her. Her lips were a tight line. Her spine ramrod straight. Her crossed arms relaying her complete disapproval. 'You're annoyed with me.'

'The team needed you to be there tonight, Gabe. Debrief is mandatory. That's what you told me a few months ago.'

Gabe rubbed his hands through his hair. 'I know. Look, I'm sorry…I just didn't feel like a post-mortem. Talking with the Fishers was hard. I just needed to be alone. To think.'

'How were they?' she asked, her stance softening.

'Distraught,' Gabe said, clenching his fists by his sides as visions of a sobbing Scott reran in his head.

Beth knew from his clipped reply that it must have been bad. He looked so tired, the subdued light in the room making the lines on his forehead look more prominent. He'd always looked younger than his thirty three years but tonight he looked every one of them and a few more. It couldn't have been easy talking to Brooke and Bridie's parents.

She felt her own weariness responding to his. His voice washed over her and with his chest looking all smooth and inviting she could feel her anger dissolving.

She had the absurd urge to lay her head against him and shut her eyes like she had in this very hotel room a few months ago.

Beth sighed. 'I know that must have been awful but all the team needed was a few words of thanks, of encourage-ment. Every single one of us felt Bridie's death too, Gabe.'

Gabe felt lousy. She was right. He'd been self-centred. There was a knock at the door. 'That'll be room service.'

Beth nodded. 'I'll go. I know you want to be alone. I just wanted you to know you have some fence-mending to do.'

'No,' Gabe said, putting a hand out as she backed towards the door. 'Don't go. I don't want to be alone. Not now you're here.'

Beth felt heat slam into her. Her legs turned to jelly, making any further retreat impossible. She had to go. The emotional roller-coaster of the marathon surgery was still too raw between them. The things he'd said to Brooke still too fresh in her mind. It was dangerous to be near him when they were both still so keyed up.

But the plea in his eyes was hard to ignore and as he brushed past her to answer the door, his male scent wafted towards her and her stomach lurched.

Gabe took the tray from the waiter and set it down on the bed. He noticed Beth still hadn't moved. She was wearing cargo pants and a T-shirt that clung to her breasts and was standing as still as a statue, looking at the bed like it was a monster from the deep.

'How about we eat on the balcony?' he suggested.

Beth knew she was powerless to say no. She'd stood beside Gabe for the last thirty odd-hours, watched while he'd valiantly tried to bring Bridie back from the brink. And he wanted her to stay and she couldn't deny him his request. The balcony was good. *Anywhere but the bed.*

She swallowed. 'As long as you put a shirt on.' She knew her voice was husky and hated herself for it, but there was no way she could sit opposite a shirtless Gabe with his sexy accent and six-pack abs and not think about how she had put her mouth on every inch of him.

The hair at Gabe's neck prickled. Beth wanted him. He felt tendrils of sensation crawl along his spine and shoot to his groin. Despite his professional façade, he hadn't stopped wanting her since their night together, and right now he wanted her more than ever.

He picked his shirt up from the edge of the bed, where he'd slung it when he'd first entered the room. He held her gaze as he pulled it over his head and dragged it down.

'Better?' he asked huskily.

No. 'Thank you,' she said, and commanded her legs to walk out to the balcony.

After some initial awkwardness they settled into small talk. Gabe drank cold beer from the mini-bar and they watched the lights of the River Cats down below, ferrying customers from one side to the other. They avoided any talk of the operation.

'I can't believe you're actually living in a hotel for seven months,' Beth said as she took in the magnificent city view.

He shrugged. 'It was part of my contract. There didn't seem to be any point renting for such a short term.'

Short term. The words reverberated around her head.

She nodded as her gaze fell on his bed. Had he brought anyone else back here? Short-term job. Short-term women? Had she been one of many?

Not that it mattered or was any of her business if he had. Or that she should be thinking about it while he talked about whatever it was that he was talking about.

'And there's this study that I'm involved in…'

His career. Right. He was talking about his career. He had a promising career on the other side of the world. She removed her eyes from the temptation and the memories of his bed, plastered a smile on her face and nodded at him encouragingly.

'I'm sorry,' he said a few minutes later. 'I'm prattling. I guess we really should be talking about the thing we've avoided taking about for too long. The baby.'

Beth felt like she was plunging down a loop on a roller-coaster as her stomach dropped. *Not tonight.* She didn't have the emotional fortitude for that.

'No.' She smiled, placing a hand on her belly. 'Let's not. Not now. It's been a big weekend and we're both tired. I don't have the stamina for a deep and meaningful conversation. Prattling's good.'

An hour later Gabe stifled a yawn as Beth told him about some local tourist spots. He remembered the overwhelming weariness from his last two separations but this time it was different. The success of those ops had offset the tiredness. He couldn't remember having felt more tired.

'I'm sorry,' she said rising to collect the plates. 'You must be exhausted. I'll go.'

No. Don't go. He didn't want to be alone tonight. Gabe shrugged, rising also, his pulse accelerating, humming along with the beat of the city spread out below them. Would she stay if he asked? 'No more than you. We've both had very little sleep in the last couple of days.'

'Yes, but you've borne the brunt of all the pressure. You broke the bad news to June and Scott. That sort of thing takes it out of you more than just physically, Gabe.'

The way she said his name felt like a caress. Like she'd stroked her hand along his belly. 'I like it when you call me Gabe,' he said softly, placing a stilling hand on hers as she reached for his empty beer bottle.

His hand felt warm and vibrant against hers. *No.* This was all wrong. This was too…everything. Too much. Definitely too much.

'Stay.'

Beth felt her mouth turn as dry as ash. A slight breeze ruffled his hair. 'No.' She moved around the table to go inside, dishes in hand, and he stepped in front of the doors, blocking her exit.

'Gabe,' she croaked.

His groin surged again at the ache in her voice as she said his name. 'Please. I need you tonight. I think we need each other.'

Beth could feel her resolve melting. Fast. 'Gabe,' she whispered. She wasn't strong enough for this. 'Don't ask me this. Not tonight.'

Gabe could see she was battling her desire. Knew that an honourable man would stand aside and let her pass. But he wasn't strong enough to deny what he'd wanted every day since that first time.

'You know you want to.'

Beth swallowed. Her eyes fluttered shut for a few

seconds. When she opened them again he'd stepped closer. He took the dishes from her unresisting fingers and set them on the table, allowing him to move closer still. She could feel his body heat enveloping her, his warm breath sweet on her face.

She watched mesmerised as his hand gently pushed back a lock of her hair that had fallen forward. His hand cupped her jaw, his thumb stroking lazily down her neck.

'Beth,' he whispered.

He was staring at her mouth and she ached to feel his lips on hers. She swallowed to moisten her parched mouth as she swayed towards him. She mustered her last remnant of sense. 'We shouldn't be doing this,' she croaked. 'Things are complicated enough.'

'Yes, they are,' Gabe whispered, his gaze not leaving her mouth. She was so close, her mouth so near he could almost taste her, and he wanted her so much his body throbbed.

'Can you walk away?' he asked softly. *I sure as hell can't.*

Beth shook her head, not sure she could articulate a response. His intense gaze on her mouth was breathtakingly erotic.

'Neither can I,' he groaned as he dropped his head and claimed her lips.

All rational thought and reasons for not doing what they were doing fled as Beth melted against him. She felt boneless and weightless and completely unable to support herself. She clung to him as his kiss plundered her mouth and ravaged her body.

He was breathing hard and she was shocked to hear her own ragged breathing match his. She sounded crazed, desperate, dragging in air as the kiss deepened and the whole world spun crazily around her. Gabe was the only thing solid and not moving and she held him tight, anchoring her body to his.

Gabe backed Beth against the glass, the scent of citrus filling his senses, igniting his desire. His need to be surrounded by her, to touch her naked skin was frantic, bordering on reckless. He yanked her shirt out of her waistband and gave a guttural groan as he felt her hands at his fly.

A siren on the street below broke through the sultry city hum and pierced through the haze of lust encapsulating them. Gabe pulled away from the kiss, placing his forehead against hers as he struggled for breath.

'Hell,' he muttered. He would have had her here. Standing against the glass where people in half of the surrounding hotels could watch them. She was tired. And pregnant.

'Gabe?' Beth whimpered, looking at him with a dazed expression, her mouth swollen and moist from their passion. Her head was spinning, her pulse echoing loudly in her head, making coherent thought beyond her. 'Don't stop.'

'Shh,' he whispered, placing two fingers against her mouth. 'Let's go inside.' He opened the sliding glass doors and held out his hand to her.

Beth took his hand without hesitation and he backed in as she followed. Their gazes stayed locked.

'This is better,' he said as the city noises receded. His calves hit the edge of the bed. 'More private.'

Beth nodded. Not that she could have cared. The sight of Gabe looking sexy as hell obliterated everything. His hair was messy and his lips were still moist from her mouth. His fly was gaping and a peak of underwear was visible past his half-untucked shirt.

She stepped closer and reached for the hem of his shirt. 'I want this off,' she said huskily.

Gabe grinned. 'On. Off. Make up your mind.'

'Off,' she said testily, frustrated by her desire to see all of him.

Gabe swallowed at the impatient demand and raised his arms above his head.

Beth inched the shirt up slowly, pressing kisses along the hard planes of his chest as she revealed more and more skin. She stroked her tongue against his nipple and smiled to herself as she heard his swift intake of breath.

Then she pulled it over his head and claimed his mouth in a deep kiss that left them both wanting more.

'My turn,' Gabe said, pulling away reluctantly.

Beth grinned and held her arms above her head. Gabe whisked her T-shirt off in one deft movement. 'My, oh, my,' Gabe sighed, staring at her lush breasts encased in delicate red satin and lace. The front clasp taunted him. 'Sister Rogers...is this what you were wearing beneath your scrubs all weekend?'

He traced the edge of the lace over the ripe bulge of her breast and Beth bit her lip as her nipples scrunched tight. 'No.' She gave a husky laugh. 'I was wearing a pale lemon one actually. I showered before I left work and changed into clean underwear.'

Gabe hadn't looked away from her breasts. He cupped the lacy mounds. They looked bigger, fuller than he remembered, The baby, he supposed. He ran his thumbs in lazy circles over the satin. He heard her breathing go ragged and felt his groin tighten as he looked at her to discover her eyes shut and her teeth biting into her bottom lip.

He traced his finger down into the dip of her cleavage and quickly unclipped her bra. Her breasts swung free and she gasped as the air hit her heated flesh. She moaned out loud when he dipped his head and took a rosy tip deep into his hot mouth.

'Gabe,' she panted.

'You are so beautiful,' he groaned as he lifted his head to claim the other nipple.

'Oh, Gabe,' she whispered, the words no more than a strangled sigh.

He raised his head to claim her mouth and she was more than a match for his ardour and passion. He sank slowly down on the bed behind him, pulling her with him until they were joined from head to hip. Her weight on him felt good as she ground her pelvis against his.

But it wasn't enough for Beth. She wanted more. She wanted to see all of him, feel all of him against her. She wriggled off him, standing a little unsteadily on her feet. He looked sexy as hell, lying on the bed before her, and she smiled at him.

'What?' He grinned.

'Just looking,' she teased.

'Come back here.' He held his arms out for her. She was naked from the waist up and her hair was tousled and her mouth looked thoroughly kissed. And he wanted her.

Beth shook her head. 'No. These off,' she said, and pointed to his jeans. She ran two fingers down his open fly.

Gabe could feel his erection strain against the fabric. 'I'll show you mine if you show me yours.'

Beth grinned. 'Deal.' Her hands flew to the buttons of her cargo pants as she watched Gabe intently. She made short work of her pants as Gabe lifted his hips and slid his jeans down.

His black cotton boxers barely contained him. 'Those too,' she ordered.

Beth felt her eyes widen as he slid his boxers off. She devoured his magnificent proportions. Her hand reached out to touch it.

'Uh-uh.' Gabe grinned, covering himself. 'You next.' He pointed to her matching red satin and lace knickers.

Beth rolled her eyes. 'Spoilsport.' But she gave a few deliberately exaggerated wiggles of her hips and slid her last article of clothing off.

'Now can I touch?' she asked, hand on hip.

Gabe chuckled and removed his hand. 'Now you can do whatever you like.'

And he gave her hand a yank, toppling her onto him. His chuckle was cut off by her mouth. She kissed him long and hard. She kissed him until they were gasping for air and their bodies demanded more.

His length pressed into hers felt divine but it wasn't enough. Beth wanted to feel more. Feel surrounded by him. Dominated by him. She rolled off and pulled him over with her. *That was better.* His weight squashed her against the bed and she revelled in her femininity as his pelvis rocked against hers.

Gabe wanted more too. He wanted to touch her. Taste her. It had been months since he'd sampled the delights of her body and he was starving for her. He trailed kisses down her neck and heard her whimper of loss.

'It's OK,' he said, kissing her mouth. Her eyes were glazed and he felt his erection surge. 'I need to kiss all of you.'

Beth needed his mouth on hers more than her next breath but she also knew what magic he could weave on the rest of her body. *Her mouth could get in line.*

She shut her eyes as he trailed kisses everywhere. Her back arched as he laved her breasts with sweet attention. Her belly clenched and she shivered as he stroked his tongue across her stomach. And when he parted her legs and put his tongue inside her she cried out his name.

'Gabe, please…' She pulled at his shoulders. 'I want you inside me.'

Gabe grinned. 'I thought I was.' He smiled as he kissed his way back up her body.

Their mouths fused as Gabe entered her. Beth groaned and wrapped her legs around his waist as he went deeper.

Gabe, sheathed to the hilt, rose up on his elbows. He didn't move, watching the ecstasy on Beth's face, her eyes closed in pleasure. He didn't want to stop doing this.

Beth felt filled and luxuriated in Gabe's possession. She moved slightly and her eyes fluttered open. Gabe was staring at her intently.

'Tell me you've wanted this since the last time.'

Heat lanced her groin. 'Gabe,' she pleaded.

Gabe withdrew the barest amount and then pulsed into her again. 'Tell me,' he demanded, his voice husky with desire.

Beth felt the craving to have him pull out and plunge in again nearly overwhelm her. She saw the desperation in his eyes. Saw the shadow of the last two days still there. She moved beneath him but he held her firm.

'Gabe, please,' she gasped. 'I need you to…'

Gabe repeated the slight movement again, knowing it was driving him as crazy as her. Fighting the urge to drive in and out of her in wild abandon. 'I've dreamt of this moment every night since that first time. Tell me you want me as much as I want you.'

'Gabe,' she panted, the sensation unbearably erotic.

He pushed into her harder. 'Tell me.'

Beth couldn't bear it any longer. She knew this was about more than their one-night stand. It was about months of denial and hungry looks, about the baby and about breaking his promise to the Fishers and failing probably for the first time in his life.

'Yes,' she gasped. 'Yes. I've thought of us a lot.'

Gabe lowered his mouth and sucked roughly on her nipple. 'Not good enough, Beth.' His voice was ragged. 'I need to hear you say you want me.' He claimed her other breast.

Beth nearly fainted from the eroticism of his teeth grating against her nipple. 'I want you, Gabe,' she whimpered. 'Damn it, I want you.'

Gabe locked gazes with Beth, the desire in her eyes ratcheting his lust up another notch. He pulled out abruptly and plunged back in again. He heard her gasp and watched as her pupils dilated with need. He repeated the movement again and again, their gazes holding steady.

'Gabe.'

He could hear the loss of control in her voice, feel her body trembling against his. Feel his own loss of control roll through him.

'Beth,' he groaned, burying his face in her neck.

'Oh, Gabe,' Beth cried, clinging to his trembling shoulders, her orgasm breaking as quickly as it had built.

'Beth, Beth, Beth,' he whispered as she broke around him and he followed seconds later.

CHAPTER EIGHT

A FEW minutes later Gabe rolled off her and stared at the ceiling.

'I'm sorry,' he said after a while as his heart rate returned to normal.

'It's OK,' she said, turning to look into his troubled eyes. 'It's been an intense couple of days.'

She held out her arms to him and Gabe went to her gratefully. He laid his head against her chest, her heartbeat bounding beneath his ear. She had every right to hate him for the stunt he'd just pulled. But after the surgery, after losing Bridie, he'd needed to feel a connection with her away from their jobs.

Their relationship had been strictly business since that first night. They'd both agreed it was the only appropriate thing to do. But they'd just been through a momentous experience together and she was having his baby, for crying out loud. Tonight of all nights as they faced their uncertain future, he'd needed to know they were more than just colleagues.

Beth cradled his head against her breast and absently ran her fingers through his hair. She tuned into his deep even breathing as the silence stretched between them. 'It wasn't your fault, Gabe. You did everything you could. We all did.'

Gabe heard her voice reverberate through her chest wall. *She could read his thoughts now?* He rolled on his stomach, his chin against her sternum, looking up into her face. 'I know that. I do. Really. I was just thinking, if only we'd had more time to prepare. If only Bridie had been stronger.'

Beth nodded. 'You played the cards you were dealt, Gabe.'

'Yes, but could I have played them better? Could I have done more?'

'Gabe,' Beth reasoned, 'do you always beat yourself up like this after something goes wrong in surgery?'

Gabe dropped his head, pressing a kiss to her chest. He lifted it again. 'I've never lost anyone during surgery. In fact nothing's ever really gone wrong for me intra-operatively. A few hairy moments but nothing I couldn't handle.' He grimaced. 'That's part of the whole Fallons-never-fail thing.'

'Oh.' Her fingers stilled in his hand. Poor Gabe had a whole legacy to uphold. 'You're human, Gabe. And human beings fail. Even your father, I bet.'

Gabe shook his head. 'Oh, no, the great Harlon Fallon never failed.'

Beth stroked a finger down his cheek and cupped his jaw. Gabe's stubble grazed erotically against her palm. 'Yes, he did. He neglected you. His own child. He failed in the worst way.'

Beth knew better than anyone how neglect bruised. How damaging it was.

Gabe gazed into her earnest blue eyes and gave her a gentle smile as he covered her hand with his. He eased it off his jaw and dropped a kiss into her palm and another on her sternum. He turned his head and laid it against her breast again, shutting his eyes as she caressed his scalp and he succumbed to the eroticism.

He opened his eyes a few moments later. The view was pretty damn good. Her pale skin sloped away down the valley between her ribs, smoothing out over her stomach and rising into crescents on either side to cover the jut of her hips.

He trailed a finger down her middle, circling her belly button, his hand coming to rest in the cradle between her hips where his baby was safely nestled. He could feel the slight bulge growing up from behind Beth's pubic bone.

He kept his hand there. His child. He had made her pregnant. Even now, a month down the track, he found it hard to wrap his head around.

'Have you felt it move yet?'

Beth's hand stilled in his hair. She wasn't used to him talking about the baby. She could feel her heartbeat become more forceful in her chest. Surely he could too? 'Some flutterings.'

Gabe waited, hoping to feel something. He barely breathed, reluctant to move a muscle in case he missed the tiniest quiver. The baby didn't oblige but just knowing that they'd created life was particularly poignant given the loss they'd both just experienced. His baby grew safe and snug beneath his hands and yet he knew too well the frailty of life.

He shifted so he was on his elbows again and turned to look at her. 'I'm sorry about how I reacted when you told me about the baby. You kind of…threw me that day.'

Beth shrugged, dropping her hand from his hair. 'I

know. For what it's worth, when I found out it kind of threw me for a while too.'

'So there was a time when you weren't so...together about it?' Gabe grinned. 'That's a relief.'

Beth smiled. 'There was some initial hyperventilating but I always, always wanted it. I've loved this baby from the start.' Beth placed her hand where Gabe's had so recently been. 'I've wanted a baby for a very long time.'

'Since you were fifteen?' Gabe asked, and wasn't surprised to see her nod. 'I guess that's understandable. I wish I could say I've had the same burning desire. But I've never felt like that. Never.'

Beth had got used to Gabe's assertion that he wanted to be around, had started mentally adjusting her plans, so his admission surprised her. Was he trying to back out? 'I've already told you I don't expect anything from you.'

Gabe saw her tense. Heard the strain in her voice. He traced a finger down the side of her face. 'I'm not trying to back out. I'm just trying to explain how...unprepared I was for this. I mean, whenever I think about being a father now and particularly after today, I think how hellish a surgeon's life can be on a child. We don't keep normal business hours.'

Beth nodded slowly, thinking about the marathon thirty hours he'd just been through. But she also remembered his whispered words to Brooke and his fight at the end to give Bridie every chance, and knew that he'd fight just as hard— harder—for their child.

His green eyes were solemn. She could see he was torn. 'We all have choices, Gabe. You can choose to break the mould.'

Gabe sighed. He pushed himself away, rolling onto his back. He remembered that night having dinner at the Winterses' house. Witnessing the balance that John had managed to strike with career and family. But was he capable of that?

'It's not going to be easy to throw everything in I've ever worked for, ditch everything that's important to me and come to Australia to play daddy.'

Beth twisted her neck to look up at him. 'I'm not asking you to.' Though, heaven help her, as the baby fluttered beneath her fingertips, she wanted it more and more.

Gabe rolled on his side and looked at her. 'Come to England with me.'

Beth shut her eyes. If her life was simple, she would. 'I can't, Gabe. You know why.'

Gabe nodded slowly. 'Tell me about him. Your son. About that time.'

Beth stared into his eyes. Maybe if he knew, he'd understand why this was so important to her. She grabbed the sheet.

'Cold?' he asked as he helped her.

She shook her head. She couldn't lie here naked and tell him about her past. Her memories would lay her bare enough. She covered herself and rolled on her side, raising herself up on an elbow to face him.

Beth was silent for a few moments, struggling with the memories. 'It was an awful time. I mean, things had been bad for so long at home but that made it so much worse. My father was furious. He pressured me to give the baby up for adoption. I didn't want to but…I was scared and powerless.'

Her tortured gaze pleaded with him to understand. 'Of

course you were,' he said quietly, stroking a finger up and down her arm.

'I was also underage. He kept telling me it was best for the baby. That I was too young to look after him. That I couldn't do it by myself. That they wouldn't support me. That the baby deserved the best start in life. Two parents who loved him. Not a teenage troublemaker. Didn't I want the best for my baby? he kept asking. He accused me of being selfish and self-absorbed. He just kept at me and at me.'

Beth remembered the arguments and the horrible tension during that time. How she'd been a virtual prisoner in her own home. How she'd cried herself to sleep every night, begging the universe for intervention that never came. How appeals to her stepmother had fallen on deaf ears and she'd felt the loss of her own mother so very acutely.

'Until I caved in.' Beth felt tears build in her eyes and blinked them away. 'Of course I wanted the best for him. He was my baby. I loved him.'

'Oh, Beth…' Gabe murmured, hearing the twenty-odd years of misery in the huskiness of her voice.

'It broke my heart when they took him away.'

Beth recalled the precious minutes she'd had to hold her baby as if they were yesterday. His smell, his newborn curiosity, looking around at the bright new world he'd emerged into. The devastation as he was taken away.

'There hasn't been a day go by when I haven't wondered about him.'

He lifted a hand and stroked a finger down her cheek. 'I'm sorry.'

Beth felt a lump lodge in her throat at his sincerity. 'I've wanted a baby ever since, Gabe. Desperately. I'm sorry it scares the hell out of you but I've been waiting for this for twenty-three years.'

Gabe nodded. They were silent for a while and Beth had never felt so exposed in her life. 'I suppose you must think my adolescent behaviour pretty shocking.'

Gabe stroked her cheek. 'Not at all. I think you were young and sad and desperate for someone to understand you. To love you.' God knew, his own adolescence had been pretty fraught.

Beth nodded. He was right. That was exactly how it had happened. She'd never thought for a minute there'd be such lifelong consequences.

'So he hasn't come forward yet...your son?'

Beth rolled onto her back, the pain in her heart rendering her incapable of supporting herself. 'No. It's been five years since he could have...contacted me...if he wanted to. But...nothing.'

'I'm sorry, Beth.' She sounded so bereft he wasn't sure how to comfort her. And he wanted to. Having her here with him tonight had been immeasurably comforting to him.

'You understand why I can't leave?'

Gabe nodded. He didn't want to, but he did. 'Have you thought about finding him yourself?'

A tear rolled out from the corner of her eye. She wiped it away. 'Yes...often. But I couldn't bear the thought of being rejected. At least if he comes to me, he's seeking me out. I'll know he wants to have a relationship.'

It didn't matter that another baby was growing inside her. Her thoughts, her arms still yearned for the child she'd held for only a few cherished moments.

'I thought maybe this birthday he'd seek me out. But...'

'When's his birthday?'

'January tenth.'

Gabe blinked. January tenth? *Click*. That date was burned into his brain. *The night they'd first made love.* Another piece of the puzzle slotted in. That was why she'd been so upset. Why she'd sobbed in his arms. It had been her son's birthday. The son she'd given up twenty-three years before.

'That was the night of the movies,' Gabe said.

Beth shot him a surprised look. He remembered the date? 'Yes.'

More and more things were making sense. It had been obvious something had been up that night. Obvious that she wasn't someone who usually slept with a man after such brief acquaintance. 'So it wasn't my pure animal magnetism?'

Beth laughed at his faux crestfallen look, grateful for the lighter mood. 'I'm afraid not. Although it was very good.'

Gabe pulled her towards him and snuggled her against him spoon fashion. He kissed her shoulder. 'Actually, I was pretty shocked when you agreed to come with me. I was certain you were going to knock me back. I'd taken you for a straight chick after about two minutes in your company.'

Beth smiled, loving the feel of his contours surrounding hers. 'Why did you even ask, then?'

Good question. Something had appealed to him despite what his instincts had been telling him. 'Nothing ventured, nothing gained. And I was feeling kind of sad myself that night and you seemed like a kindred spirit.'

Beth kissed his arm. 'Your dad?'

He nuzzled her neck. 'My dad.'

They were silent for a few moments and Beth trailed her fingers up and down his firm biceps. She laced her fingers through his. 'You were exceedingly lucky that you got me on that day,' she mused.

'So if it had been the day before or the day after?'

'You wouldn't have stood a chance,' she confirmed.

'Well, I don't know.' Gabe grinned, kissing the curve of her neck, 'I can be very persuasive.'

'So I've discovered.'

Gabe grinned as he trailed a hand down her side, following the dip of her waist and the rise of her hip, and settled it low on her belly. He nuzzled his face into her neck, inhaling her unique Beth scent. Her hair smelled like citrus and her skin like soap and sated female.

He became aware of a slight stirring beneath his fingers. He stopped nuzzling, his head stilling as he realised he was feeling foetal movements. His baby's movements. 'Is that what I think it is?' he asked.

Beth felt goose-bumps feather her neck as his breath fanned her skin. She moved her hand down to cover his so their fingers interlocked. 'Yes,' she said huskily.

Gabe felt incredibly connected with her as they lay sharing the wonder of the moment. He felt truly torn. How could he not want this? It was his child. What kind of a father could be part of such a moment and feel so conflicted? Shouldn't it be clear cut?

'I wish I knew what to do about this,' Gabe whispered, feeling completely out of his depth.

'It's OK, Gabe,' Beth whispered, removing her hand and reaching behind her to stroke his cheek. 'This wasn't exactly on your agenda. You came here on a seven month contract to separate conjoined twins. Not to have a baby with a woman you hardly know. It's OK to not have the answers.'

Her words made him feel even worse. 'I know you,' he protested.

She removed her hand. 'Yes, but not like people who usually make babies together do.' Although, given their short acquaintance, he knew her better than most people she'd worked with for years did. 'There's no commitment. You don't love me, Gabe.'

Beth stalled, amazed at how the realisation hurt. She hadn't expected or needed his love but lying here, cradled against him, the L-word between them, she knew she wanted it. Knew as surely as the sun would rise in the morning that she wanted it as much as the baby growing inside her.

'Neither do I want you to be,' she said automatically, while her brain grappled with the mind-blowing revelation. *This was bad. Really bad.* Not only had she gone and got herself pregnant by him, she'd done something even more stupid. She'd gone and fallen for him. A hotshot, didn't-even-live-in-the-same-hemisphere neurosurgeon whose skills did not include relationships, particularly fatherhood.

'You've still got a few months on your contract and we can use that time to figure out how we're going to work this.'

Gabe was touched by her generosity. He wished he could lay out a plan for her but things were still a big jumble inside him. His entire focus until now had been on the separation. But feeling the tiny movements beneath his hand had highlighted his biggest responsibility yet and how out of his depth he felt.

'You're being very understanding about this.'

Beth felt like a fraud. If only he knew—discovering she

loved him had completely blown her mind. She was on total autopilot. 'A lot's happened in the last few months,' she dismissed. 'In this last weekend. The separation. Bridie.' *And I love you.* That had happened too.

Lying here with him, his hand over her womb, she wondered how she'd been so blind for so long. Especially as now she could pinpoint the exact moment she'd fallen. That first night as he'd rocked her while she'd sobbed her heart out—that had been the moment. She'd been so miserable that day and his gentleness and consideration had touched her more deeply than she'd known.

'You can play whatever part you want in this baby's life, Gabe. There's no pressure. You've still got a few months in the country and now the separation's done, you're freer to think about it.'

Gabe dropped a kiss on her shoulder. 'Thank you, Beth. For everything. For being so understanding and for everything you did for the Fisher case.'

Beth smiled and snuggled in closer. 'I would like to tell my family…if that's OK. I'm not going to be able to hide it for too many more weeks anyway.'

'Of course,' Gabe assured her, not feeling so assured himself. Was he ready for this to go public? But what right did he have to put the brakes on her joy? She'd been more than sensitive to his struggles. 'Stay?' he murmured.

Beth's heart banged crazily in her chest as her love for him swelled to excrutiatingly painful proportions. *She should go.* But he'd asked her to stay. And lying snuggled in the arms of the man she loved while their child lay inside her was too tempting.

She turned in his arms. 'Yes.' *Just a few more hours.*

Their love-making was different this time. Light. Flirty. After the intenseness of the previous time and the seriousness of the last forty-eight hours, laughing and rejoicing in each other's bodies was just what the doctor ordered. They drifted to sleep an hour later totally sated, completed exhausted, smiles on their faces.

Beth called in to the PICU to visit Brooke on her way to work on Tuesday morning. Memories of last night, telling the Winters clan about the baby, curved the corners of her mouth. They had all been so thrilled and she almost skipped into the unit.

Scott was sitting in a recliner at the bedside, an alert-looking Brooke, her head still bandaged, snuggled into his chest. June gave Beth a long hug.

'I'm so sorry about Bridie' Beth murmured.

'We know.' June smiled, her eyes shining with tears. 'We know everyone did all that they could.'

Beth squeezed June's hand as she squatted beside the chair. Brooke was looking pinker and less puffy than when she'd last seen her. Her chest was criss-crossed with a jumble of tubes and wires, her cheeks and nose largely obscured by brown tape where the nasal prongs and feeding tube were secured.

'Look at you,' Beth crooned. 'No breathing tube. You're so clever.'

Beth held out her hand and watched as Brooke's gaze followed and then fixed on her proffered finger. The little girl reached out a tiny hand and grasped it, smiling a toothless grin.

'Nothing wrong with her.'

Gabe's voice was deep and sexy, his accent giving her goose-bumps as it oozed across the distance between them.

'G-Gabe,' she said, looking over her shoulder. Gabe shot her a smile and it went straight to her internal muscles, lancing them with the heat of erotic memories.

'Beth.'

'What do you think of our girl?' Beth asked turning her attention back to the surviving Fisher twin as her pulse rate tripped. If only it wasn't just lust she saw in his gaze.

'I'm cautiously optimistic.'

Beth laughed. 'Do you hear that, sweetie? High praise indeed.'

Scott and June laughed and Gabe joined them. It had been twenty-four hours since he'd kissed her goodbye at his hotel door and he realised he'd missed her. His sleep had been haunted by her face all night. Disjointed snippets of him pushing her on a swing. Them laughing. Her belly swollen with his child.

Beth stood. 'I'd better go. I'll call in later,' she said, addressing June.

'We'd like that,' June said.

The bed area was crowded with four adults and Gabe stood aside so she could get past him. 'See you later,' he murmured as she brushed by.

Beth faltered, his accent and unique scent seducing her to stay longer. Maybe rub her face into his shirt. She barely acknowledged his comment as she fled on trembling legs.

A few hours later Beth sat in her office with David, trying to concentrate on his first evaluation. He'd come in on a day off. As NUM it was her responsibility to appraise all the students. They looked at his written objectives before commencement and assessed his progress.

She went over his scrub sheet and they talked about the different procedures he'd been involved in and mapped out some more objectives for the remaining months.

'You're going really well,' Beth said, wrapping it up. 'You've put in a lot of extra hours. I've given you top marks here, as you can see. I only wish there was a column for ability to catch fainting NUMs. I would have scored you top there as well.'

Beth laughed and David gave her a nervous smile.

'Oh, come on, David, relax.' Beth grinned. 'That was a joke. You're supposed to laugh.'

'Sorry.' David cleared his throat.

Beth looked into the student's face. 'You don't seem yourself today. Everything OK?' she asked, shutting his file.

He gave her another nervous smile and she raised her eyebrows at him, encouraging him to say whatever it was that was obviously still on his mind. They sat for a few moments looking at each other.

'David, was there something else you wanted to discuss?' she prompted.

'Actually, yes…there was.'

Beth watched him shift uncomfortably in his chair. He looked very uneasy. What the hell could he want? Had someone been bullying him? Had he witnessed something sensitive? She gave him an encouraging smile. 'So…'

'Oh, dear,' he said at last. 'I've thought of this moment for such a long time and now it's here I feel all tongue-tied.'

Beth gave him a puzzled look. What on earth was he talking about? 'It's OK,' she said. 'Just spit it out.'

He nodded. 'OK. I think…actually, no, I know. I'm… your son.'

CHAPTER NINE

BETH heard the words come out of his mouth but couldn't actually believe she'd heard them. It was as if everything outside her office had ceased to exist and she and David were sitting in a little bubble, the only two people on the planet.

Could it be true? She desperately wanted to believe it. Had her son finally made contact?

'If this is a joke...' Beth said, finally finding her voice.

'No,' David said, giving his head an emphatic shake. 'The agency gave me the details that you left on record and I have these.' He reached down, dug through his backpack and handed her a small bundle.

She took it, her heart pounding in her chest. Her own strong, neat handwriting stared back at her. They were letters. She didn't have to open them to know they were the ones she'd written him over the years.

'You got these?' she whispered, her eyes filling with tears.

'Yes. Mum and Dad were always up front about me being adopted.'

Beth drank in the sight of him. His height, his blondness, his broad strong shoulders, his long fingers. *Her son.*

Her son had sought her out. She clutched the edge of her desk as her arms ached to embrace him.

'I've imagined this moment since the day they took you from me. I've rehearsed what I would say. But now it's here, I can't think of a single word.'

'It's OK,' David grimaced. 'It's taken me two months to work up the courage.'

'How…how did you know where I worked?' The details she had on record were a name, home address and phone number only.

David shrugged. 'I knew you were a nurse from your letters. I think, actually, deep down, that was my impetus to become one. When I got your details last year—'

'You only got them last year?' Beth interrupted, trying not to feel too hurt. She'd always hoped that her son would have been so eager to know her that he'd contact the agency straight away. But he hadn't.

David nodded and continued. 'It wasn't difficult to track you down after that. When we got to choose our practical electives, I put the General's operating theatres as my top choice.'

'Why didn't you contact me at the number the agency gave you?'

He shrugged. 'I guess I wanted an opportunity to get to know you first.'

Beth frantically tried to think back over the last months. What kind of an impression had she made? She knew she'd developed a good rapport with him but it had been painstakingly collegial. Especially after Gabe's teasing comments. Had she been too distant? Heaven only knew what he thought of her.

Beth's head spun. People bustled by in the corridors either side of her office. She could hear the clatter of instruments as someone walked by with a tray and a trolley being pushed past. She couldn't believe she was sitting in her office with her long-lost son and the world hadn't ground to a halt.

'I suppose you want to know why I did it? Why I gave you up?'

David stood. 'No. I don't. Really.'

What? Surely he must want to now? Surely he'd be curious? Beth opened her mouth to protest. She needed to tell him. She had to explain.

'Look, you obviously had your reasons,' David said. 'You must have been very young. Whatever they were doesn't matter to me. Sure, I went through a long period in my teens when I wondered about you. A lot. Wished you were around. Felt kind of disconnected and rootless. But I always knew deep down you did what you did out of love for me.'

Beth nodded, a lump in her throat making words impossible. Her heart ached, knowing that he'd thought of her. Knowing that he longed for her as much as she'd longed for him. She wanted to weep for his troubled years. It didn't matter that many teenagers went through the same thing. She'd given him up so his teens would be less troubled than hers.

'I'm sorry you went through that. Sorrier than you'll ever know.'

'It's OK,' he dismissed. 'I've matured. I can look back and say I've had a pretty good life.'

Part of Beth was relieved to hear him validate her painful decision. To hear that her sacrifice had been worth it. But part of her wanted to say, *I could have given you a good life too.*

'So do you mind me asking why it took you so long to contact me?' Beth asked.

'I travelled for a few years after I finished school. I think I was trying to find myself. It was good for me. I went to a lot of poorer countries. It put my own petty troubles into perspective. I guess I came away with a bit of a what-will-be-will-be attitude. That things happen if they're meant to happen. After that I started nursing and I don't know if I ever would have sought you out except then I met Andrea.'

Well, thank you, Andrea. Beth didn't know who she was but if she ever got to meet her, she was going to kiss her feet. The thought that this moment might never have arrived was too awful to contemplate. 'Your girlfriend?'

David nodded.

'So Andrea thought you should seek me out?'

He shook his head. 'We've both started to talk long term. I mean, I love her. I know I want to be with her for ever. You know…wedding bells and the pitter-patter of tiny feet.'

Beth blinked. He seemed so young to be so responsible and mature.

'Andrea had a brother who died ten years ago from cystic fibrosis. She carries the gene. And I realised that I don't know anything about my genetic history. I mean, not just about whether there's CF in my genetic make-up. Nothing at all.'

David has sought her out for medical reasons? Beth felt winded as she clenched her hands into fists beneath the desk. She wouldn't have thought such practicality would hurt so much. But it did. It wasn't how she'd pictured this day at all.

A question about his genes was natural, she supposed, but she'd been hoping for something along the lines of— reconnecting with the woman who had given him life. His practicality was like salt being rubbed into wounds that had never fully healed.

'Er, right…' she said, grappling for some perspective, trying to see this from his side. Grateful for anything he was giving her but wanting more. Wanting it all. This was all new to both of them. There wasn't a guide book. She had to let him lead the way. After all, he didn't owe her anything. She'd given up any claim on him and his life when she'd signed the adoption papers.

'Well, there's no CF in my family or in any of the extended family, as far as I know. In fact, I'm pretty sure there are no major genetic illnesses at all.'

'What about my father?'

Beth swallowed. 'I don't know… I'm sorry. I only knew him very briefly.' Someone who had offered her comfort and solace in a world that had been full of uncertainty and conflict. 'I can give you a name if that helps.' She cringed. What must he think of her? Was he judging her?

David shook his head. 'It doesn't matter.'

Would he ever give her a chance to explain the circumstances surrounding his conception and the terrible years that had led up to it? Or the pain of her decision that had left a permanent bruise on her soul?

'I really have to get going,' David said, checking his watch. 'I've got a class starting in half an hour.'

Beth stood. *So soon?* She didn't want him to go.

'Oh…all right, then.' *Let him lead.* She came out from behind her desk. 'Do you think we could…get together away from work some time? I'd like to talk a little more…maybe get to know you?'

'Ah…I'm not sure… Maybe. I'm still wrapping my head around all this.'

Beth knew that feeling. She saw him cast a furtive glance towards the door and took a step closer to him. 'I'd hate to lose contact now.' She placed a hesitant hand on his arm.

'Maybe,' he repeated.

Beth was dismayed when he took a step back and her hand fell from his arm. It was too much. She was rushing him. He'd come to find out his genetic make-up, not play long-lost son. She swallowed a lump of emotion burning like a hot coal in her throat. *Let him lead.*

'Thank you,' he said.

Beth stood aside so he could pass. She balled her hands into fists lest they try and reach for him again. It took all her self-control not to burst into tears and beg him to stay. He paused in the doorway.

'Do you regret you ever had me?' he asked.

He didn't turn so she was forced to address his back. 'The only thing I regret is giving you up,' she said, her voice husky with barely contained tears.

And then he walked out the door and Beth collapsed into the nearby armchair, giving the wall of emotion that had been building inside her its inevitable release. Tears spilled down her cheeks as the enormity of what had just happened hit her squarely in the solar plexus.

The event she'd been waiting twenty-three years for had finally arrived. Her son had reached out to her. And if the meeting hadn't exactly followed the script she'd written in her head for years—it had been a start.

Gabe bustled into Beth's office a few minutes later and found her sitting very still, her eyes red-rimmed.

'Beth?' He crouched beside her. His heart beat frantically in his chest. *Had something happened with the baby?* 'What's wrong?'

Gabe's concern cut through her turmoil. She turned glistening eyes on him. 'Oh, Gabe,' she whispered. 'He was here. My son was here.' She forgot all about professional behaviour and promptly burst into tears, her head falling against his broad shoulder.

'Hey,' Gabe soothed, his hand automatically going to the nape of her neck, his thumb rhythmically stroking the sensitive skin there. 'Shh,' he murmured.

He let her cry, not asking any of the questions that were crashing through his head. 'It's OK,' he whispered. 'It's OK.'

Beth felt the wave of her outburst slowly subside. She left her face pressed into his neck as she fought for control. Firstly because she was so embarrassed she'd cried all over him—again. *This was becoming a habit!* Only this was in broad daylight and they were at work. And also because he smelt so good.

'I'm sorry,' she apologized, reluctantly leaving the shelter of his neck.

Gabe pulled some tissues out of the box on her desk and offered her the swathe. 'Here.'

He stood while she blew her nose and dabbed at her eyes as she prowled around her small office. He sat on the edge of her desk and swung his leg as Beth pulled herself together.

'What happened?' he asked.

'It's David,' Beth said, still pole-axed by the revelation.
Gabe frowned. 'David? The student nurse?'

Beth nodded her head slowly. 'Pretty amazing, huh?'
She filled him in on their conversation, noting Gabe
seemed as stunned by the turn of events as she was.

'I always thought he was interested in you. I just got the
motivation wrong,' Gabe mused as he watched her worry
at her bottom lip. 'You seem a little anxious.'

'It wasn't exactly the loving reunion I'd hoped it would
be. What if he doesn't want a relationship with me?'

'Give him time, Beth. It took him four and a half years
to make contact with the agency and two months to break
the news to you. It's obviously not in his nature to be rushed.'

'I know, I know,' she said. 'You'd think I could be
patient after all these years of waiting. But there's been so
many wasted years. I don't want to waste any more.'

Gabe pushed himself off the desk and stood in front of
her. He placed his hands on her shoulders. 'Let him come
to you,' he said gently. 'Don't push him. He may not be a
confused teenager any more but he's bound to have issues
of trust and identity. There's no doubt still a bewildered
little boy lurking behind his mature exterior.'

Beth looked into Gabe's serious gaze. She knew he was
right. She sighed and nodded, placing her head against his
chest. He pulled her close and she allowed herself the
luxury of a brief embrace, her heart swelling at his tenderness. Maybe the wait would be more bearable if Gabe was
around to share the burden?

She felt so good in his arms that she knew she could stay
here for ever. Why did she have to love someone who
didn't love her back?

Beth drew in one more lungful of Gabe pheromones and broke away, returning to her seat, struggling for normality. 'I'm sorry, forgive me. Was there something that you wanted?'

Gabe shut his eyes, holding onto the sweet memory of their nearness for a second longer. He turned to face her, their intimacy scattering. 'The media office has been bombarded with calls for a press conference.'

'Scott and June have already released a statement.'

'They want to talk to the team.'

Beth thought for a moment. 'What does John think?'

'He thinks it's a good idea. He's set it up for tomorrow afternoon. I want you there.'

Beth blinked, her heart skipping a beat at his emphatic request. 'What for?'

'All the main players are going to be there. You headed the nursing team as well as looking after all the theatre logistics. We couldn't have done it without you. They might want to talk to you.'

It sounded very sensible when he put it like that but part of her had hoped he'd say, *Because I want you by my side*.

She sighed and flipped her diary to the next page. 'What time?'

Beth gathered in the wings of the auditorium stage with the rest of the medical staff at two the next afternoon. Scott and June were there also and she chatted with them while they waited for the media to assemble and set up.

'Right,' John Winters said, calling the crowd to order. 'I will kick off the conference with a prepared statement. Mr and Mrs Fisher will then field questions before we hand over to Gabe and the surgical team. Everyone will give a brief overview of their part in the process and then there will be more questions.'

Satisfied everyone was on the same page, John led the team out onto the stage, in the middle of which was a long table. Eight chairs and eight glasses of water were set out evenly and everyone took their pre-planned positions as the flashbulbs of a hundred cameras dazzled them. Behind them the General's corporate logo decorated the back wall.

Beth took the end seat, partially blinded by the lights shining down at them. She could vaguely see that an audience had gathered in the terraced theatre-style seating before them. She knew that Hailey was there somewhere, although the lights made it impossible to make anyone out.

The next hour flew in a haze of camera flashes and a barrage of questions. As always, Beth was impressed with Gabe's leadership. He rejected any suggestions that the operation had been a one-man show and deflected questions equally to all members of the team, giving them praise and credit for the roles they'd all played.

For her part, Beth answered the questions that came her way and the few more Gabe kicked straight to her. It wasn't something she felt particularly comfortable with, especially given the loss of Bridie, and she was grateful when things appeared to be drawing to a close.

'Dr Fallon,' a reporter somewhere near the back called, 'you've had a stellar career with two previously successful separations. Given that one of the babies died, do you think this will dent your reputation?'

Beth frowned and squinted, trying to see past the lights to who'd asked such an impertinent question. Was the man trying to imply that his reputation meant more to him than the life of a child?

'I'll let my reputation speak for itself.'

Beth could hear the tightness in Gabe's voice and knew the question had annoyed him.

'Can you tell us a bit about what the differences were with this op and the last two?' another reporter called.

Gabe rattled off an explanation of the differences, their unique anatomies and Bridie's weakened state being the major one.

'As the son of a highly successful Nobel Prize-winning medico, don't you feel, with only Brooke surviving, that you've failed, Dr Fallon? That the surgery was a failure?'

Gabe couldn't really see the face of the persistent reporter, which was probably just as well. He prepared to throw the journalist a noncommittal reply. Comparisons with his father were inevitable.

Beth's blood was boiling and she'd opened her mouth before she'd given it proper thought, beating Gabe to the punch.

'I think I can speak for all of us, including Scott and June, in saying that Dr Gabriel Fallon is a brilliant neuro-surgeon who undertook a highly complex procedure in less than ideal circumstances.'

What would the dog-with-a-bone reporter know about the life-and-death decisions people like Gabe made every day?

'I'm sure failing in your job means not meeting your deadline or screwing up a quote. Failing in our business has much more serious ramifications. Patients die and that's a hell of a lot more critical than some headline in a two-bit rag.'

How dared he bandy the word around so liberally?

'I'm sure not even the great Harlon Fallon could have pulled off the outcome we were all hoping for. But nobody worked harder than Gabe Fallon to achieve it.'

The room fell silent. The background murmur ceased. The clatter of lenses stopped. Their retinas were even given a reprieve from the constant flare of flashes. She could see David sitting up at the back but she had no time to process his presence as the entire gathering turned their attention on her.

What are you all looking at? Beth wanted to hurl at them, acutely embarrassed by her outburst, her hands automatically shielding her stomach. She was tired. And pregnant. And in love. And her long-lost son had turned up. And they were messing with Gabe. *She really didn't have the patience for this.*

John Winters recovered first. He'd been shocked to find out about Beth's pregnancy and even more so to learn that Gabriel Fallon was the father. He shouldn't have been surprised to hear his daughter defending Gabe so eloquently. *So much for just being friends.* He pointed to a female reporter in the first row and the show got back on the road with an anaesthetic question for Don Anderson.

Gabe glanced down the line as he leaned forward to take a sip of water, still stunned by Beth's caustic defence of him. She was sitting with her hand covering her belly, her cheeks still tinged with colour, looking like she was hoping the floor would open up and swallow her.

And there was the biggest difference, he realised. Beth. Beth, working with him efficiently in the background. Beth, scrubbing in beside him, anticipating his needs. Beth, ordering him to sleep. Beth, telling him enough, Bridie had

had enough. Beth, staying with him. Beth, sobbing in his arms. Twice. Beth, carrying his child. Beth, understanding.

She'd been the difference. In a few short months she'd become an important presence in his life—constant and steady. From the very first moment, the emotional vulnerability behind her reserved façade had intrigued him. Today, leaping to his defence, she fascinated him even more.

Oh, no. He was falling in love with her!

CHAPTER TEN

BETH couldn't get away from the press conference quickly enough. She wasn't sure who had read what into her little outburst but she wasn't sticking around to answer any more prying questions. She'd barely slept a wink last night after David's bombshell and combined with the little sleep she'd had at the weekend, she wasn't in the mood for petty hospital speculation.

She castigated herself again. She had no doubt her outburst would be juicy gossip this time tomorrow. She might as well have stood up and said, *I love him, back off*. Wait until they found out she was pregnant! She couldn't hide it for ever—another month, maybe two at a stretch. What would they think then?

Beth headed for the main entrance doors. She needed some air. And coffee.

Hailey, Gabe and David rode down in the lift together.

'I didn't realise you were in the audience,' Gabe said to David to distract him from his raging thoughts and Hailey's speculative gaze. How the hell had Beth achieved the one thing no woman had done? And what on earth was he supposed to do about it?

David shrugged. 'My shift had finished. I thought I'd have a sticky beak.'

Hailey looked at Gabe expectantly and it took a second for him to fathom the raised-eyebrow look. He performed the introductions distractedly.

'This is Beth's sister, Hailey,' he said. 'David is one of the student nurses in Theatre at the moment.'

Gabe watched David surreptitiously as the light dawned that Hailey was his aunt. He looked uncomfortable, like Beth had after her outburst during the press conference. Like he'd give anything to be anywhere else.

Gabe felt for the young man. He knew how it was to feel estranged from someone who had given you life and how your identity suffered. But surely he must realise that it hadn't been easy for Beth. If David kept rejecting a relationship with her, it would break Beth's heart. And he couldn't bear the thought of that.

He suspected David was kidding himself. Why had he been at the press conference if he truly wanted nothing more than medical details from his mother? Why all the weeks of seeking her out like an eager puppy, spending as much time with her as possible?

He figured David was just as curious about Beth as Beth was about her son. He just needed encouragement. He could at least do that for the woman he loved. Because he was damn sure anything else was beyond him at the moment. Loving her. Being a father. He didn't know how to do any of those things.

'How about we all go get a coffee?' Gabe suggested.

'Sure,' Hailey chirped.

'Nah, I got to get home,' David said as the lift doors opened onto the ground floor. 'I'll grab one to go, though.'

Beth was at the counter when Gabe, Hailey and David joined her. Her head was pounding and for the second time in her entire working life she contemplated leaving early. She just wanted to crawl into bed and sleep for a week and come back when the talk had died down.

'Hey, you,' Hailey greeted Beth.

'Hi!' Beth turned, plastering a smile on her face that slipped immediately she noticed Gabe and David standing behind her sister. She quickly re-fixed the smile on her face, the throb in her head kicking up a notch as she nodded at her son and her lover.

'Woohoo,' Hailey teased. 'That was quite a performance, Beth. Lucky none of the press knew you and Gabe are having a baby.' She paused to pat her sister's stomach.

'Hails,' Beth warned, knocking the hand away, her gaze flying to David's face.

'Oh, come on.' Hailey laughed. 'A juicy bone like that? The operation would have been totally forgotten.'

'Hailey!' Gabe interrupted abruptly. He too turned to look at David.

'David,' Beth said, reaching a hand out to her son, who was backing away from the circle and looking at her like she'd grown a second head.

'I…I have to go,' he stuttered.

'David…no!' Beth exclaimed as he turned and ran.

Hailey turned to Gabe as Beth ran after David. She looked at him confused. 'Er…am I missing something?' she asked.

Gabe sighed. 'It's…complicated,' he said as he witnessed

Beth catching up with David and managing to halt his flight. He could see how panicked she looked and wished there was something he could do to fix things. His heart swelled with love at her dilemma and it tore him up to know that there was nothing he could do. He wanted to go to her side but knew neither of them needed his interference.

'David, wait,' Beth called finally catching his sleeve and pulling. Her pulse was skittering madly. *Damn Hailey and her impulsiveness!*

'It's OK,' he said, shrugging her off.

'I wanted to tell you,' Beth said, breathing from the exertion of her short run.

'You don't owe me any explanations,' he said. 'Anything you owed me you gave away when you gave me up.'

'No, David,' Beth pleaded, her heart breaking. The look of shock on his face betrayed the confidence he had exuded yesterday. Gabe had been right—there was obviously still an insecure little boy inside. 'I only found out about you yesterday, I didn't want to dump it straight in your lap.'

'I understand,' he said, turning away. 'You have other priorities now.'

His accusation cut when Beth knew it wasn't true. She searched for the right words. 'I have enough love for both of you,' she implored.

David inspected her face for what seemed an age and then backed away again.

'I have to go,' he said.

Beth felt as if the walls were caving in around her and ran after him as he fled. She didn't hear anything other than the sound of her heart beating through her skull, intensifying the throb of her headache. David crossed a narrow internal road and she followed him without thinking, desperate for him to understand, her eyes glued to his retreating back.

She rubbed at her forehead as her foot landed on the bitumen. Her head throbbed as her pulse banged through her temples. She didn't hear the car. She didn't see the car. All she knew was that suddenly it was there and its brakes were squealing and the wheel was turning, but it was too late.

She was vaguely aware of Hailey screaming as she turned to protect the baby. The slow-moving hatchback struck her on the back of the legs. She felt her hip hit the bonnet and winced as her body rolled across the front of the car. In the blink of an eye she'd slid off the other side and was falling to the ground. Her head struck the bitumen as she landed on her side on the road. And then she didn't hear or see anything. Everything went black.

'No!' Hailey screamed.

'Hell,' David whispered.

'Beth!' Gabe yelled, and was running before she even hit the ground. Hailey and David moved a second later.

Gabe reached her first, rounding the now stopped car, and was at Beth's side in an instant. His heart pounded in his chest as her inert form chilled him to the core.

'Oh, God, Beth,' Hailey sobbed, throwing herself on the ground beside her sister.

Gabe felt for a pulse and was relieved to feel a strong carotid. He looked up at David, who was staring down at his mother, pale and shaken.

'Beth!' Hailey cried again.

'Is she OK?' An elderly man knelt beside Gabe. A laceration on his forehead was bleeding and he was clearly dazed. 'I'm so sorry. She just stepped out in front of me,' he muttered.

'It's OK, sir, we know,' Gabe assured him, while Beth's failure to regain consciousness scared the hell out of him.

He took a second to assess the situation. Hailey was practically hysterical, David visibly shocked and the driver obviously traumatised. And he'd never felt more scared in his entire life. The woman he loved had been hit by a car—he wanted to vomit.

Beth murmured and he wanted to sweep her up in his arms and kiss her, but the doctor in him knew she could have serious injuries—broken bones, internal injuries, head trauma—not to mention the baby. *Hell, the baby!* His thoughts crystalised as his hands moved to support her neck. It was imperative she didn't move.

'Hailey,' Gabe said, his voice loud and commanding to cut through the sisterly hysteria. He used one hand to give her shoulder a firm shake. 'Run to Emergency. Get help. I need a trolley and a neck brace. Take him.' He gestured to the driver. 'He'll need checking out. Hurry.'

Hailey saw the urgency in Gabe's gaze and the wave of panic receded. She sniffed and nodded, rising to do his bidding.

'David.' Gabe looked up at the young man who still hadn't moved, his sheet-white face aghast. 'David!' Gabe called again, his voice stern in an effort to snap David out of his stupor. 'I need a hand here,' he said abruptly.

David nodded, his daze clearing as he sank to his knees. 'I didn't mean to—'

'I know,' Gabe said curtly, realising how awful David must feel but too concerned about Beth to be nice.

'Will she be OK?' he asked.

Gabe heard the crack in his voice. *He damn well hoped so.* 'I'm sure she will,' he said, taking pity and nodding with a confidence he didn't feel. 'The car wasn't going very fast.'

Beth groaned and moved her hand to her temple. She hurt everywhere. *What the hell happened?*

'It's OK, Beth,' Gabe whispered, leaning close, his hands still supporting her neck. His nausea was receding and he was so relieved to see her coming round that he wanted to weep. 'You're OK, lie still. Help's coming.'

Beth cracked open an eye and saw David leaning over her, his face worried. She wanted to stroke his brow and soothe away the lines, but pain stabbed into her eyeballs and she shut her eyes. 'What happened?' she muttered.

'A car hit you,' Gabe murmured quietly. 'What hurts?'

The memory returned, the sickening moment of impact, and she groaned. 'Everything hurts.' Her hands, through habit, moved to her stomach. The baby. Oh, God, the baby.

Beth's eyes flew open and she tried to move her head to look down at her stomach. Gabe's hands tightened their hold on her neck.

'Lie still,' he commanded.

'The baby,' she protested. 'Gabe, the baby.' Sudden tears sprang to her eyes and her voice cracked. 'I can't lose this baby.'

Beth reached out to David as her full memory of the preceding events returned. She knew the news had hurt him. Even through her throbbing head and raging thoughts she wanted to reassure him that he wasn't being replaced.

'I can't lose either of my babies,' she whispered, and was so grateful when he squeezed her hand that she started to cry.

They were interrupted by the arrival of a team from Accident and Emergency. No less than the director of the department Ben Stapleton, two orderlies and Rilla. And, of course, Hailey. There was flurry of activity.

'Rilla,' Beth cried, reaching for her sister's hand. Hailey took the other one. 'I need an ultrasound straight away.'

Rilla nodded. 'Be careful, she's pregnant,' she said to the team as they rolled Beth onto a spinal board.

They had her inside the department in ten minutes, an IV in two minutes later and a barrage of tests ordered. The General looked after its own and the NUM of Theatres and daughter of the Chief of Staff was top priority.

'Ultrasound,' Beth said to Ben. 'I need to have the baby checked out.'

'On its way,' he confirmed. 'After that we'll get some X-rays.'

'No.' Beth tried to shake her head but it was secured in a neck brace. 'No X-rays.'

'Beth,' Gabe said softly.

'No X-rays,' she said firmly. 'I'm fine.'

'You are not fine. You've been hit by a car. You were out cold for a couple of minutes.'

Beth gave her limbs a shake. 'I'm fine. Nothing hurts.' She winced. 'More than anything else,' she clarified. 'Nothing's broken.'

'You could have some cracked vertebrae.'

'I don't have pins and needles or numbness in my peripheries. My back and neck aren't sore.'

'You could have fractured your skull,' he said, pointing to the bloodied graze near her temple.

'Listen to him, darling, he's making perfect sense,' an imposing voice interrupted.

'John,' Beth said, smiling as her father pushed through the curtain. She accepted his embrace. 'Who called you? Go back to work. I'm fine.'

'I did,' Gabe said. 'I was hoping he'd pull rank.' Seeing her back to her old in-control self was comforting but she'd scared the hell out of all of them. He wouldn't be happy until everything had been checked out.

'Be sensible, darling. We X-ray pregnant women every day. All care will be taken. Doesn't your head ache?'

'It ached before I got hit,' Beth dismissed. 'All I need is the ultrasound.'

The head of the radiology department popped his head through the curtain. 'Beth Rogers, are you making a scene?'

Beth grinned at the consultant. 'Gordon. This is service. You'd better have the ultrasound machine with you.'

Gordon pulled the curtain back to reveal the ungainly mobile machine. He looked at the crowded cubicle—six adults and a cumbersome piece of equipment were not going to fit. 'I think we need some space in here, folks.'

'Yes, absolutely,' John agreed. 'Gabe, you stay with Beth. Come on, everyone else out.' He noticed David hovering at the back. 'I don't think we've met, young man. John Winters. I'm Beth's father.' He held out his hand and David shook it. 'Thank you for helping out. You probably don't have to hang around now.'

'No!'

Everyone turned and looked at Beth.

'I want him to stay,' Beth said, justifying her vehement rejection. She held out her hand to him and held her breath. 'David's my son.'

Beth only had eyes for David as he walked tentatively towards her and took her hand. She didn't care that by tomorrow not only would the entire hospital know she was pregnant but that she had a twenty-three-year old son.

She turned her gaze to her stunned family. 'He's family. I want him to wait with you.'

It took a few seconds but John, unflappable as always, recovered first. 'Of course, darling,' he said gesturing to David. 'We'll all go and wait outside. Together.'

Beth noticed David hesitate. He'd gone from complete anonymity to full exposure in twenty-four hours. Was he ready for her family? He'd sought her out only through a sense of genetic curiosity and she'd spectacularly outed him. Would he run a mile? Had she totally blown it?

'Actually, I think I'll head on home…now that you're OK… Andrea's expecting me.'

Beth swallowed. *She'd blown it.* David looked like he wanted to run screaming from the room. A new mother. A new sibling. And now an entire new family. Her heart throbbed as painfully as her head as he extricated his hand from hers.

'Of course.' Beth forced a smile onto her face as Gabe's words echoed in her head. *Don't push him.* 'I'll see you later?'

Beth tried not to come across as too desperate, too needy, but the thought of losing contact with him again was unbearable. David gave a noncommittal nod and her heart broke a little as she watched him leave the cubicle. What had she expected? That her banged-up body would make up for years of angst?

Beth lay on the trolley, her gaze firmly fixed on the spot where David had disappeared through the curtains, a hand down low on her stomach. Every part of her body ached and she fought the urge to cry.

'OK,' John said, rounding everyone up, his daughter's misery palpable. 'Let's give Gordon some room to work.'

Everyone trooped out until there were just the three of them. Gabe's heart swelled with love at Beth's obvious heartache and he covered her hand with his. She looked at him with an injured gaze and he gave her hand a squeeze.

'Give him time,' he murmured as he leant forward and kissed her gently on the forehead.

'OK, then,' Gordon said, interrupting their moment. 'Let's check out this baby.'

Beth pulled up her top and shimmied her trousers down a little. The gel was cool against her skin as Gordon placed the transducer on her abdomen. He fiddled with some buttons and the screen flickered to life.

The second their baby appeared on the screen Gabe knew he was lost. It looked like a skeletal alien. All large skull and bones. But he loved it as surely as he loved the woman who carried it. How could he think about a semi-involved role when he was desperately in love with both of them?

'Well, the little tike's certainly kicking a lot,' Gordon murmured. 'What's the gestation?'

'Nearly nineteen weeks,' Beth replied huskily. It was too much. This day had been too much. An emotional roller-coaster that had looped her around until her head spun. And now this. Meeting her baby for the first time.

'Nice strong heartbeat,' Gordon said.

Gabe saw the strong central flicker of his baby's tiny heart. He swallowed hard as a block of emotion rose in his chest. His throat felt tight and he felt like the walls were closing in on him. What sort of a father would a career-orientated neurosurgeon make? What if he screwed it up, like his father had?

'Have you had your routine scan yet?' Gordon asked.

'No, it's booked for next week,' Beth said, unable to drag her gaze away from the monitor.

'I'll just have a quick look at the placenta then we may as well check everything out.'

Beth nodded absently, totally mesmerised by the picture on the screen. She felt another kiss pressed onto her forehead and glanced up a Gabe. He seemed equally entranced by the image and for the first time she began to hope that everything was going to be OK.

'Placenta's intact,' Gordon said. 'Looks like the impact didn't affect the baby at all.'

Beth smiled, her hand trembling as the dark cloud of worry miraculously lifted. 'Really?'

'Really.' Gordon nodded. 'There are no signs of any separation or evidence of haemorrhage. But you need to take it easy for the next few days and see someone straight away if you start to bleed.'

Beth tried to nod but the collar prevented any vigorous movement. Anything. She'd do anything to keep Gabe's baby safe. 'Of course.'

'We'll admit her for observation,' Gabe commented above her head. 'That way we can be sure she's getting bed rest.'

Beth looked up at Gabe. 'Hey,' she said, 'I won't jeopardise this baby's health, Gabe.'

'I know. This will just make it easier for you.'

Beth opened her mouth to protest but Gabe's expression brooked no argument.

'You scared the living daylights out of all of us. You will be admitted.'

She shut her mouth. She could hear the echo of real fear in his voice. She could actually think he cared if she wasn't too careful. But then she thought how awful it must have been to witness someone being hit by the car and realised he'd be as concerned about anyone.

The next half-hour flew by as Gordon looked at the developing baby from every angle. Everything was structurally normal and the baby was growing well. It was certainly active. Beth followed its movements as it moved back and forth. The next twenty weeks stretched before her interminably. She was impatient to hold her baby in her arms.

She risked a look at Gabe. His expression was unfathomable. Had he given too much away earlier when he'd admitted how frightened he'd been? Was he as awed as she was by the sight of their baby or was he changing his mind, desperately trying to think of ways to hightail it back to the UK? She wished she knew what he was thinking.

'Do you want to know the sex?' Gordon asked.

Beth looked at Gabe, her eyebrows arched.

Gabe looked at her and shrugged. Did he? He was too involved already. 'I don't know—do you?'

Beth nodded. She did. Suddenly she wanted to know desperately.

'Girl,' Gordon announced.

A girl. Beth's heart swelled with love. Would she have her father's peridot eyes and caramel hair? Or the same dimple in her chin as her big brother?

Beth grinned at him and Gabe was struck by an image of a little version of Beth. Blonde pigtails and pink ribbons, a little bow mouth and blue, blue eyes. The vision was captivating and he was alarmed by how much it appealed. He didn't know how to be a father to a delicate little girl. He didn't even have a sister.

The ultrasound ended and Gabe left quickly to find her family. Beth brooded while he was gone. She had no idea what Gabe felt about having a daughter.

The arrival of everyone back in the cubicle, including a worried Penny, distracted her from her thoughts.

'Oh, my God. I came straight away,' Penny wailed as she gave Beth a huge hug.

Everyone spoke at once, wanting to know about the accident and the ultrasound and David, and Beth's head throbbed. She suddenly felt a hundred years old. She just wanted to sleep.

Gabe could see the growing weariness in every line of Beth's body. He felt a little overwhelmed himself—no wonder David had hightailed it out of here. The Winters clan was full on. He wasn't used to being around a family that was so tight-knit. His upbringing seemed very…cold in comparison. Still, it was good to know that his child, his daughter, would be surrounded by all this love. By people who cared. By women—lots of women. That's what girls needed, didn't they?

'I think Beth needs some rest,' Gabe said, cutting through the din. 'Let's get her admitted so she can get into bed.'

'Admitted? I thought you said she was OK?' Penny turned to John.

'Just to be on the safe side and because she's refusing X-rays,' Gabe hastened to assure Penny.

Beth shot him a get-over-it look but was exceedingly grateful that he was taking control. It had been a big day. A big few days.

The operation.

Sleeping with Gabe. Again.

Discovering her love for him.

David.

Being knocked flat by a car.

She was so weary she could sleep for a week.

CHAPTER ELEVEN

AN HOUR later she was ensconced in a private room with a spectacular view of the Brisbane skyline. She could also see Barney's and could make out a couple of her staff heading across the road towards the welcoming neon sign.

Her family had just left and she was blissfully alone. The neck brace Gabe insisted she still wear was annoying and she shifted to get comfortable in it. She sighed and shut her eyes. The crisp hospital sheets felt heavenly against her aching body. There was so much to think about so much to process, but within seconds she was drifting away into the blissful folds of slumber.

Gabe found her sound asleep half an hour later. He'd left her in the capable hands of her family earlier. His head was grappling with the revelations of the day and he'd needed some time and space to deal with them. Not that anything seemed any clearer.

He moved into the room and pulled a chair up beside her bed. She looked awful. Her pale skin looked even more so against the backdrop of the white sheets. A dark purple bruise had formed over her right temple and he knew by morning it would spread to encompass her entire right eye area.

She was so still and he felt fear grip him again as his heart rate picked up. His gaze zeroed in on her chest, concentrating on its rise and fall, counting her deep, even respirations. His fingers strayed to the pulse at her wrist and he breathed out, reassured by the strong beat.

His hand shook as he withdrew it, his head playing a rerun of the accident. He saw her being struck by the car, rolling across the bonnet and crashing to the ground. The image of her motionless, crumpled body would be forever implanted on his retinas. He'd thought she'd been killed. His heart still beat madly in his chest hours after the event when he thought about that awful fleeting moment.

That would be a cruel twist of fate. Realising he'd found the one woman who'd managed to get beneath his defences, only to have her snatched away less than an hour later.

She lay with both hands cupped low on her abdomen in a pose peculiar to pregnant women worldwide. Even in sleep she was protecting their child. His hands itched to join hers but he didn't want to disturb her and his feelings were still too jumbled to let his guard down.

Today he'd fallen in love with a woman and met his daughter. It had been momentous, to say the least. And none of it had been on his agenda. God, he could hear his father mocking now. Harlon Fallon would be rolling in his grave to hear a son of his actually thinking about putting family first.

But beliefs ingrained over years cautioned him against diving in head first. How many relationships had he seen break up in his line of work? How many kids played second fiddle to the job? Like he had? Was it fair to act on a whim when he wasn't sure if he was equipped to go the distance?

Was it fair for his daughter to have to settle for being second fiddle?

Looking at Beth lying so still and silent he knew he loved her more than anything. Loved her enough to wonder if she and the baby would be better off without him. She'd already told him she was perfectly happy to do it herself. Maybe he needed to heed that. What made him think she'd even want him anyway? She had what she wanted—a baby. And her son back. Did she even have room in her life for him?

His pager beeped and he quickly pushed the silence button. He needn't have bothered. Beth didn't stir. He checked the message. It was the PICU. He'd been expecting their page. They were removing Brooke's dressing and he'd asked to be notified.

He left Beth's side reluctantly, the dictates of his job warring with his desire to be with her. This was what it would be like all the time if he got involved. Constantly feeling guilty for neglecting one or the other.

He strode down the corridors, eating up the distance between Beth and Brooke with long powerful strides, his head seething. His duty to be with the injured woman he loved at odds with his duty to his patient.

'Hi, June,' he said, plastering a smile on his face as he approached Brooke's bedside.

'Hi, Gabe.'

'So, how's that head looking, sweetie pie?' Gabe crooned, turning his attention to Brooke who gave him a big smile.

Erica Hamel from the plastics team was there also and they were both pleased with how the wound was looking. They spent twenty minutes discussing the next steps in the process for Brooke. Gabe checked his watch several times. He wanted to be there when Beth woke up.

'So, that was quite a press conference,' June said after Erica had left.

'Yes.' Gabe smiled.

'You need to employ Beth as your publicist,' June teased. 'I think she's a bigger fan than even me or Scott.'

Gabe looked at June. There was a shrewd gleam in her eyes. He chuckled. 'Some would say that reporter had it coming.'

'Oh. Absolutely.' June laughed. 'If Beth hadn't said something, I was about to.'

Gabe laughed. 'Well, thanks, I think I can stick up for myself.'

'You shouldn't inspire such loyalty if you don't want your honour defended.'

Is that why Beth had done it? Out of loyalty?

'Of course, I think there was a bit more than loyalty involved,' June said.

Gabe shot June a polite smile. Could she be right? Was there something more that had motivated Beth's outburst? He excused himself, telling June he'd pop into see Brooke in the morning.

He was back at Beth's room eight minutes later, stopping abruptly in the doorway when he realised Beth wasn't alone. David sat in a chair beside the bed, his back to the door.

Gabe approached quietly, crossing to the opposite side of the bed.

'Oh.' David rose. 'Hi. I was just… I'll go,' he said.

Gabe reached across the bed and laid a stilling hand on

the younger man's arm. 'Please, don't. Beth would want you to stay.'

David looked at him and Gabe could almost touch his aura of indecision and conflict. It seemed they would make similar company tonight. Gabe pulled up a chair and was relieved when David resumed his seat.

They sat watching Beth breathe for a long time. Neither of them spoke. It was as if they were both just content to see signs of life.

'So…it's been a big couple of days,' Gabe said eventually.

'You can say that again.' David grimaced.

'You do know how much it means to Beth to have you back in her life?'

David nodded. 'I don't know if I can be what she wants.'

'She just wants a chance to get to know you. That's all. She's your mother—'

'I have a mother,' David rejected quickly. 'I wasn't just on loan to the woman who raised me for the last twenty-three years, you know. Beth can't surely expect us to have the same sort of mother-son relationship.'

Gabe nodded. The younger man's confusion was palpable. He was pretty sure Beth would take whatever David had to offer, but he could sense the younger man had been pushed too much for one day. 'So why are you here?'

David sighed. 'I…don't know. There were so many times as a kid that I wondered about her. Wondered why. How she could have given up her child. And when things were messed up I used to think…to know she'd be able to make it right. But then I grew up and I realised she must have had her reasons and I'd had a good life and what would we really have to say to each other?'

David stopped and Gabe waited for him to continue. He could tell there was so much more David wanted to say.

'But when she was lying there today and she was so still, all I could think was I never got to know her. I was scared stiff she was dead and I didn't get a chance to tell her…I loved her.'

Gabe nodded. Hadn't he had just the same wake-up call? It was important suddenly to try and make David understand about Beth. David was, after all, going to be his daughter's big brother. Hopefully, for Beth's sake, a big part of the baby's life. He knew Beth well enough to know that she just wasn't whole without David.

'Giving you up broke her heart, David. Give her a chance.'

David shook his head. 'She's not going to have time for me now. She has the baby.'

Gabe clenched his hands. David had been put into a situation he hadn't expected and his confusion was more than understandable. But he was wrong if he thought Beth's love was so fickle.

'Love doesn't divide, David. It multiplies. You and Beth are halves of each other's whole. Neither of you are complete without the other. There's a hole in her life that only you fill. No one, not even another child, can fill that space.'

Gabe watched as David seemed to take his words on board.

'Get to know her. You won't regret it. If today demonstrates anything, it's that life's short. My father died without me ever really making an effort to get to know him, and that's just not right. And now I'm about to be a father myself and if there's one thing I've learned in the last little while it's that the bond between a parent and a child is too basic to us as humans to deny.'

Gabe felt the hypocrisy of the words even as he said them. *Do as I say, not as I do?* Here he was urging David to get to know Beth and yet he was contemplating some part-time father status while he still kept an eye on his career.

David nodded and they sat in silence for a while longer. Gabe's brain was working overtime. How stupid had he been? He knew how awful it had been, growing up without a father or one who'd had no emotional investment in him whatsoever. Was that what he was condemning his child to?

Would she lie in bed when she was old enough and wonder about him as David had about Beth? And what would be his excuse when she wanted to know why he hadn't given more? He wasn't a fifteen-year-old from a broken home. Somehow he didn't think *I was too busy with my career to give a damn* would cut it. He'd seen her on the screen today, had felt his heart swell with love for the tiny fragile life. He was fooling himself to think he could just go through the motions.

Everyone had always said he was just like his father. Driven. Focused. Determined. But they were wrong. He wouldn't sacrifice the woman he loved or his child on the altar of his career. He didn't know how but he'd make damn sure there was room in his life for them all.

Just because he'd had a lousy role model it didn't mean it wasn't possible. His father may have been a world-famous doctor but he had been a lousy human being and Gabe didn't intend to follow in those footsteps. John Winters had succeeded. More than succeeded.

David stood. 'Tell her I was here,' he said. 'I'll call again tomorrow.'

Gabe nodded. 'Please, do.' He reached across the bed and offered David his hand. 'She'll like that.'

The two men shook hands and David departed. Gabe sincerely hoped David would be true to his word. He couldn't bear to think of the woman he loved hurting. Looking at her bruised face was making him sick to his stomach. Her broken heart was too much to bear.

It was almost dawn before Beth stirred. She came awake slowly, conscious of every ache and pain. She felt as if her body had been on the rack. Her temple throbbed and her eye felt like it was bulging out of her head. Her stomach grumbled and the baby was kicking like crazy, no doubt demanding that her mother eat.

She brought her hand to her face and tentatively felt the swelling there. Ouch. She had a very bad feeling it was already three different shades of purple. She was going to look very scary for a few days. She opened her sore eye, pleased to find it was still possible and her vision didn't seem to be affected.

Her hand felt heavy and numb and she felt a tremor of alarm as Gabe's warning about a spinal injury reared its ugly head. Beth looked down, no easy task with the collar limiting her range of movement, to check out why. For a brief second her heart stopped. Gabe's head rested against her hand.

He'd stayed?

Beth drank in his features. His eyes were shut, his stubble making him look rakish in the subdued hospital lighting. She wanted to freeze this moment. In this instant she could almost believe they were a couple. A family. The fact that she looked like the bride of Frankenstein and his career was his first priority seemed completely inconsequential.

Her other hand hovered above his head, the urge to rumple his caramel waves almost overwhelming. But the pins and needles in her trapped hand were becoming quite painful, almost a match for the throb in her temple, and she reluctantly removed her hand as gently as she could.

'What?' Gabe roused instantly, his head snapping up.

'It's OK,' she croaked. Her throat felt dry and she swallowed. 'My hand was sore.' She flexed her fingers to encourage the circulation to return.

'Oh, sorry.' He smiled. 'I must have fallen asleep.'

Beth felt herself responding to his sleepy grin and his drowsy voice. She was sore, hungry and no doubt exceedingly frightening to look at, yet her hormones roared to life.

'You should go home, Gabe,' she whispered. 'Have you been here all night?'

He nodded rubbing at a crick in his neck. Her eye looked even worse than it had earlier, and he felt ill all over again, thinking how close he'd come to losing her the previous day. He wasn't leaving until he'd got some stuff off his chest.

'David was here earlier.'

Beth sat forward and then winced, before dropping back against the pillows. 'Really?'

'Easy,' Gabe said.

'Why didn't you wake me?'

'Beth, you scared us both silly yesterday. You were exhausted. Neither of us wanted to disturb you.'

She heard the fear in his voice again and tried not to read too much into it. 'What did he say? How did he seem?'

'He said when he saw you lying on the ground unconscious he thought you were dead and he realised he'd never had the chance to get to know you.'

Beth felt hope flower inside her as tears sprang to her eyes. 'He did?'

Gabe nodded. 'He did. He said to tell you he'd be back to see you later today.'

A tear spilled from an eye and trekked down her cheek. Could it be true? Could her son be taking his first steps towards a permanent relationship? 'Oh, Gabe, I want that so much.'

He smiled at her as he brushed the moisture from her cheek. 'I know,' he whispered. 'I know.'

Beth's mind rushed ahead and she felt a ball of nervousness tighten in the pit of her stomach. *Please, don't let me mess it up.* 'Oh, god, I must look a fright,' she fretted, touching her swollen eye.

'You're alive.' He picked up her hand and kissed her palm. 'Trust me, for an awful moment yesterday none of us thought that was possible.'

Beth's palm tingled and she looked down into his earnest gaze. He was staring at her so intently her belly flopped. 'I'm sorry I scared everyone,' she said huskily.

'Just don't ever do it again, OK?'

'OK,' she whispered. He was still looking at her with those green eyes and she wished she knew what he was thinking. Was this just a concerned friend? A father worried about his baby? Or was this a lover talking?

She couldn't bear to have him look at her like this, so...possessively, if it meant nothing. 'You should go. Get a few hours' sleep in a proper bed. You've got an afternoon list today.'

And just like that she was back-in-control Beth. The Beth that ran the General's operating theatres with efficiency and expertise. The Beth that would manage motherhood with one hand tied behind her back. The one that would be perfectly fine without him. Only he wasn't so sure how fine he'd be.

'I need to talk to you first.'

Gabe had come over all serious and Beth felt a wave of panic rise from the pit of her stomach. She didn't want to hear him talking about future arrangements. Not now. She was tired and aching. She wasn't strong enough. 'Gabe, I'm really not up to much at the moment.'

'Please.'

Beth shivered at the rawness in his tone. 'Gabe,' she pleaded.

Gabe hardened his heart to her plea. He had to say this. 'I was sitting in that press conference yesterday—'

'Oh, God. Look, I'm sorry about that,' Beth interrupted. She cringed, thinking how deranged she must have sounded. 'I don't know what came over me. I was rude and hasty.'

She was trying to take it back? What did that mean? He shook his head—it didn't matter. They weren't in high school, his feelings hadn't changed.

'I…loved it when you said those things.'

Beth's heart stood still in her chest for a few beats. He'd said the L-word.

'In fact, listening to you defend my honour, I realised that I'd fallen in love with you. I don't know when it happened—I think it just kind of sneaked up on me. And I thought, Hell, that's a complication I don't need.'

Beth's heart raced in her chest now. Had he just used the L-word again? In relation to her?

Her hand lay by her side and he picked it up and cradled it against his face.

'And then you got hit by that car and it was the worst moment of my life. And then I saw the baby…my baby.' He placed his hand low on her abdomen. 'And I didn't think it was possible to feel such instantaneous emotion. And I knew I was getting in deeper.'

Beth was holding her breath now. His palm felt amazingly possessive against hers. Was there a 'but' coming?

'And then I was talking to David and telling him how important it was to know the people who had given you life, and I realised I was being a hypocrite. That if I gave any less than my all I was condemning my child to the same fate.'

Beth swallowed. What was he saying? 'Gabe.'

'No, hang on.' He shook his head. 'I want our daughter…' he gave her hand a squeeze '…to know her father. I want to be part of her life. And I realise that you don't need me and I'm not in your parenting plan, but I can't walk away. That's something my father would have done. And I'm not my father. Neither do I want to be. I want to be a father to my daughter. In every sense of the word.'

Beth's brain fizzed with information. Maybe it was the knock to her head but she was finding it all a little hard to process. She was still stuck back at the L-word.

'Beth?' he prompted a minute later. She hadn't said anything. She was just looking at him, clearly confused.

'I'm sorry, did you just say…that you loved me?'

Gabe nodded.

Beth blinked. Truly deep down she'd always felt unworthy of anyone's love. How could someone love her when she'd given her child away? But right now she dared to feel a flare of hope.

'And that you want to be a father?'

He nodded again.

Beth's pulse trebled before she could put the brakes on. 'But what about your career? Your practice in the UK? These things are important to you, Gabe.'

'Yes, they are. And I can have them here.'

Beth still refused to give in to total elation. 'Aren't you worried how you'll manage a career and family? You're the one who told me it didn't work.'

Gabe nodded. 'I'm terrified that I'll get it wrong and I'll make mistakes, but I'm more terrified of how empty my life will be without you in it. I can't promise it'll all be plain sailing, but I can promise I'll always put you and the baby first. Always. Just like John. And Scott and June. Just because my father messed it up, it doesn't mean I will. He was never committed enough. But I am.'

He laid both hands against her stomach. 'I promise on the life of our daughter that I will be committed to make this work every day of our lives.'

Beth couldn't believe what she was hearing. He loved her and wanted to be with her. If it was true, if this gorgeous, successful man truly loved her, despite her baggage, then maybe, just maybe she could start loving herself. Forgive herself.

'I know this is a shock.'

'You can say that again.' Beth gave a half-laugh.

'I realise it'll probably take me a while to win your favour but I'm hoping you'll eventually grow to love me too and we can get married.'

'Oh, Gabe.' It was all too much. Beth felt a wave of emotion well in her throat. 'I can't believe you're proposing to me when I look like I've been pulled through a hedge backwards.'

Gabe smiled and kissed her hand. 'You're alive. I've never seen you more beautiful.' He removed his hands and laid his head against her stomach.

Beth knew tears were coursing down her cheeks but didn't care. She ran a hand through his hair, luxuriating in the feel of it beneath her hands and the weight of his head against her womb.

'Are you sure, Gabe? Really sure? Can you love someone who gave away her child?'

Gabe looked up into her tear-stained face. 'What you did was brave and completely selfless. You were a mixed-up fifteen-year-old and you put his needs first. I love you especially for that.'

Beth's eyes welled with a fresh batch of tears. 'I love you too, Gabe Fallon. I've loved you since that first night when I was so sad and you rocked me in your arms.'

Gabe felt hope for the first time. 'Really?'

Beth nodded. 'Really. And I will marry you and I will keep you to your promise to put me and the baby first. You can count on that.'

Gabe chuckled. 'I have no doubt.' He stood and sat on the edge of her bed. 'You mean it? You really do love me?'

Beth wiped away her tears. 'Really. I really do.'

'You know you've just made my day.' He grinned as he leaned closer. 'God, I want to kiss you very badly at the moment.'

Beth laughed and then winced as it reverberated through

her facial muscles. 'Right—black eye and hard collar. I must look so appealing.'

Gabe grinned. 'I think this is the for-better-or-worse part.'

Beth sobered. She raised a hand to cradle his jaw, his stubble grazing erotically against her palm. 'Are you sure, Gabe? You're giving up a lot here.'

'I'm not giving it up. Just changing direction. It'll take a while to wind things up at home but I've never been surer of anything in my life.'

She caressed his lips with her thumb. 'I love you,' Beth whispered, hardly able to believe she could actually say it to his face. She opened her arms and he went into them.

He gently laid his head against her chest where her heart beat solidly, careful not to hurt her while fighting the urge to crush her to him.

'I love you too,' he murmured against her neck.

And he knew he was going to spend the rest of his life showing her just how much.

EPILOGUE

IT WAS a fine cool winter's day in Brisbane when Beth and Gabe finally tied the knot two months later in a small civil ceremony in the Botanic Gardens. Paperwork and several trips back and forth to England had held them up but nothing had derailed Gabe's determination to get married before the baby was born.

Beth wore a cream, princess-line gown, which accentuated her twenty-eight-week bump. She had a garland of flowers in her hair and a matching posy in her hands. A spectacular peridot necklace adorned her slender neck and complemented her square-cut peridot and diamond ring. Peridot had rapidly become her favourite stone.

'You may kiss the bride,' the celebrant intoned.

Gabe grinned down at his wife. 'At last,' he whispered, and claimed Beth's mouth in a possessive kiss that told all and sundry she belonged to him.

The Winters clan clapped and cheered and then rushed forward to congratulate the newlyweds in a noisy flurry of hugs, kisses and excited exclamations.

Beth held her hand out to David and Andrea and she

accepted her son's embrace gratefully. 'Thank you for coming,' she said huskily.

'He's a great guy,' David said. 'I'm happy for you.'

Beth felt tears spring to her eyes. They'd been making tentative steps towards each other these past couple of months and she'd been so thankful. Andrea and Gabe had been encouraging and with their help she and David were slowly bridging the gap.

'Thanks for coming, you two,' Gabe said as he approached, giving Beth a hug from behind. He held out a hand to David.

'Look after my mother,' David said, grasping Gabe's hand in a firm grip.

Gabe nodded. 'I will cherish her always.'

David nodded as he and Andrea were pulled away by Penny. The extended family had welcomed David and Andrea into the fold with open arms and while there had been some challenges, they were all working together to overcome the obstacles.

'Did you hear that?' Beth whispered, turning in her husband's arms. 'He called me his mother.'

'Yes, darling,' Gabe said, dropping a light kiss on her nose.

'I didn't think this day could get any more perfect,' she said, staring up at her handsome husband, her mind still reeling from David's acknowledgement.

'Stick with me, babe,' Gabe teased. 'Every day is going to be more perfect than the last. That's a promise.'

0608 Gen Std HB

Pure reading pleasure

JULY 2008 HARDBACK TITLES

ROMANCE

The De Santis Marriage *Michelle Reid*	978 0 263 20318 9
Greek Tycoon, Waitress Wife *Julia James*	978 0 263 20319 6
The Italian Boss's Mistress of Revenge *Trish Morey*	978 0 263 20320 2
One Night with His Virgin Mistress *Sara Craven*	978 0 263 20321 9
Bedded by the Greek Billionaire *Kate Walker*	978 0 263 20322 6
Secretary Mistress, Convenient Wife *Maggie Cox*	978 0 263 20323 3
The Billionaire's Blackmail Bargain *Margaret Mayo*	978 0 263 20324 0
The Italian's Bought Bride *Kate Hewitt*	978 0 263 20325 7
Wedding at Wangaree Valley *Margaret Way*	978 0 263 20326 4
Crazy about her Spanish Boss *Rebecca Winters*	978 0 263 20327 1
The Millionaire's Proposal *Trish Wylie*	978 0 263 20328 8
Abby and the Playboy Prince *Raye Morgan*	978 0 263 20329 5
The Bridegroom's Secret *Melissa James*	978 0 263 20330 1
Texas Ranger Takes a Bride *Patricia Thayer*	978 0 263 20331 8
A Doctor, A Nurse: A Little Miracle *Carol Marinelli*	978 0 263 20332 5
The Playboy Doctor's Marriage Proposal *Fiona Lowe*	978 0 263 20333 2

HISTORICAL

The Shocking Lord Standon *Louise Allen*	978 0 263 20204 5
His Cavalry Lady *Joanna Maitland*	978 0 263 20205 2
An Honourable Rogue *Carol Townend*	978 0 263 20206 9

MEDICAL™

Sheikh Surgeon Claims His Bride *Josie Metcalfe*	978 0 263 19902 4
A Proposal Worth Waiting For *Lilian Darcy*	978 0 263 19903 1
Top-Notch Surgeon, Pregnant Nurse *Amy Andrews*	978 0 263 19904 8
A Mother for His Son *Gill Sanderson*	978 0 263 19905 5

MILLS & BOON®
Pure reading pleasure

0608 Gen Std LP

JULY 2008 LARGE PRINT TITLES

ROMANCE

The Martinez Marriage Revenge *Helen Bianchin*	978 0 263 20058 4
The Sheikh's Convenient Virgin *Trish Morey*	978 0 263 20059 1
King of the Desert, Captive Bride *Jane Porter*	978 0 263 20060 7
Spanish Billionaire, Innocent Wife *Kate Walker*	978 0 263 20061 4
A Royal Marriage of Convenience *Marion Lennox*	978 0 263 20062 1
The Italian Tycoon and the Nanny *Rebecca Winters*	978 0 263 20063 8
Promoted: to Wife and Mother *Jessica Hart*	978 0 263 20064 5
Falling for the Rebel Heir *Ally Blake*	978 0 263 20065 2

HISTORICAL

The Dangerous Mr Ryder *Louise Allen*	978 0 263 20160 4
An Improper Aristocrat *Deb Marlowe*	978 0 263 20161 1
The Novice Bride *Carol Townend*	978 0 263 20162 8

MEDICAL™

The Italian's New-Year Marriage Wish *Sarah Morgan*	978 0 263 19962 8
The Doctor's Longed-For Family *Joanna Neil*	978 0 263 19963 5
Their Special-Care Baby *Fiona McArthur*	978 0 263 19964 2
Their Miracle Child *Gill Sanderson*	978 0 263 19965 9
Single Dad, Nurse Bride *Lynne Marshall*	978 0 263 19966 6
A Family for the Children's Doctor *Dianne Drake*	978 0 263 19967 3

MILLS & BOON®

Pure reading pleasure™

AUGUST 2008 HARDBACK TITLES

ROMANCE

Virgin for the Billionaire's Taking *Penny Jordan*	978 0 263 20334 9
Purchased: His Perfect Wife *Helen Bianchin*	978 0 263 20335 6
The Vasquez Mistress *Sarah Morgan*	978 0 263 20336 3
At the Sheikh's Bidding *Chantelle Shaw*	978 0 263 20337 0
The Spaniard's Marriage Bargain *Abby Green*	978 0 263 20338 7
Sicilian Millionaire, Bought Bride *Catherine Spencer*	978 0 263 20339 4
Italian Prince, Wedlocked Wife *Jennie Lucas*	978 0 263 20340 0
The Desert King's Pregnant Bride *Annie West*	978 0 263 20341 7
Bride at Briar's Ridge *Margaret Way*	978 0 263 20342 4
Last-Minute Proposal *Jessica Hart*	978 0 263 20343 1
The Single Mum and the Tycoon *Caroline Anderson*	978 0 263 20344 8
Found: His Royal Baby *Raye Morgan*	978 0 263 20345 5
The Millionaire's Nanny Arrangement *Linda Goodnight*	978 0 263 20346 2
Hired: The Boss's Bride *Ally Blake*	978 0 263 20347 9
A Boss Beyond Compare *Dianne Drake*	978 0 263 20348 6
The Emergency Doctor's Chosen Wife *Molly Evans*	978 0 263 20349 3

HISTORICAL

Scandalising the Ton *Diane Gaston*	978 0 263 20207 6
Her Cinderella Season *Deb Marlowe*	978 0 263 20208 3
The Warrior's Princess Bride *Meriel Fuller*	978 0 263 20209 0

MEDICAL™

A Baby for Eve *Maggie Kingsley*	978 0 263 19906 2
Marrying the Millionaire Doctor *Alison Roberts*	978 0 263 19907 9
His Very Special Bride *Joanna Neil*	978 0 263 19908 6
City Surgeon, Outback Bride *Lucy Clark*	978 0 263 19909 3

MILLS & BOON®
Pure reading pleasure™

AUGUST 2008 LARGE PRINT TITLES

ROMANCE

The Italian Billionaire's Pregnant Bride *Lynne Graham*	978 0 263 20066 9
The Guardian's Forbidden Mistress *Miranda Lee*	978 0 263 20067 6
Secret Baby, Convenient Wife *Kim Lawrence*	978 0 263 20068 3
Caretti's Forced Bride *Jennie Lucas*	978 0 263 20069 0
The Bride's Baby *Liz Fielding*	978 0 263 20070 6
Expecting a Miracle *Jackie Braun*	978 0 263 20071 3
Wedding Bells at Wandering Creek *Patricia Thayer*	978 0 263 20072 0
The Loner's Guarded Heart *Michelle Douglas*	978 0 263 20073 7

HISTORICAL

Lady Gwendolen Investigates *Anne Ashley*	978 0 263 20163 5
The Unknown Heir *Anne Herries*	978 0 263 20164 2
Forbidden Lord *Helen Dickson*	978 0 263 20165 9

MEDICAL™

The Doctor's Bride By Sunrise *Josie Metcalfe*	978 0 263 19968 0
Found: A Father For Her Child *Amy Andrews*	978 0 263 19969 7
A Single Dad at Heathermere *Abigail Gordon*	978 0 263 19970 3
Her Very Special Baby *Lucy Clark*	978 0 263 19971 0
The Heart Surgeon's Secret Son *Janice Lynn*	978 0 263 19972 7
The Sheikh Surgeon's Proposal *Olivia Gates*	978 0 263 19973 4